MOTHER MASON

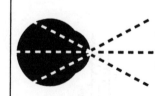

MOTHER MASON

BESS STREETER ALDRICH

Thorndike Press • Thorndike, Maine

6224463

Thorndike Large Print ® All Time Favorite Series edition published in 1993 by arrangement with Dutton, an imprint of New American Library, a division of Penquin Books USA Inc.

The tree indicium is a trademark of Thorndike Press.

Set in 16 pt. News Plantin by Juianita Macdonald.

This book is printed on acid-free, high opacity paper. ∞

Library of Congress Cataloging in Publication Data

Aldrich, Bess Streeter, 1881–1954.
　　Mother Mason / by Bess Streeter Aldrich.
　　　　p.　cm.
　　ISBN 1-56054-502-X　(alk. paper : lg. print)
　　1. Family—United States—Fiction.　2. Large type books.
I. Title.
[PS3501.L378M6　1993]
813'.52—dc20　　　　　　　　　　　　　　　　　　　93-17772
　　　　　　　　　　　　　　　　　　　　　　　　　　　　CIP

MOTHER MASON

CONTENTS

CHAPTER I

MOTHER'S DASH FOR LIBERTY

Mother sat in front of her Circassian walnut dressing table, her f—, no, *plump* form enveloped in a lavender and green, chrysanthemum-covered, stork-bordered kimono, and surveyed herself in the glass.

Mother was Mrs. Henry Y. Mason, and in Springtown, Nebraska, when one says "Henry Y." it conveys, proportionately, the same significance that it carries when the rest of the world says "John D."

It was eleven o'clock at night, which is late for Springtown. Mother had set her bread before climbing, rather pantingly, the wide mahogany stairs. There is something symbolical in that statement, illustrative of Mother's life. She had been promoted to a mahogany stairway, but she had clung to her own bread making.

Three diamond rings just removed from Mother's plump hand lay on the Cluny-edged cover of the dressing table. These represented epochs in the family life. The modest little diamond stood for the day that Henry left bookkeeping behind and became assistant cashier. The middle-sized diamond belonged to his cashier days. The big, bold diamond was Henry Y. as president of the First National Bank of Springtown.

Mother was tired and nervous to-night. She felt irritable, old, and grieved — all of which was utterly foreign to her usual sunny disposition.

She took off the glasses that covered her blue eyes. It was just her luck, she thought crossly, that she couldn't even wear eyeglasses. They simply would not stay on her nose. Deprecatingly she wrinkled that fat, broad member. Then she removed and laid on the table a thick, grayish braid of silky hair that had formed her very good-looking coiffure, and let down a limited, not to say scant, amount of locks that were fastened on as Nature — then evidently in parsimonious mood — had intended.

With apparent disgust she leaned forward under the lights that glowed rosily from their Dresden holders and scanned the features which looked back at her from the clear, oh, *very* clear, beveled glass. She might have seen that her skin was as fair and soft and pink as a girl's, that her mouth and eyes showed deep-seated humor, that her face radiated character. But in her unusual mood of introspection she could find nothing but flaws. The eyes looked weak and nearsighted without their glasses. The chin — like a two-part story, that chin gave every evidence of stopping, and then to one's surprise went merrily on. She leaned closer to the glass.

"Well," Mother said dryly, reaching for manicure scissors, "that is *the limit!*" Living with a houseful of young people as she did, Mother's English had in no way been neglected.

Then, as though to let Fate do its worst, and looking cautiously around — for she was very sensitive about it — Mother took from her mouth a lower plate of artificial teeth. Immediately, out of obedience to nature's law that there shall be no vacuum, her soft lower lip rushed in to fill the void.

"Pretty creature, am I not?" she grumbled.

Just at this point, we opine, every one will say, "Ah! No doubt the president of the First National Bank is showing symptoms of being attracted elsewhere!" Not so. Mother had only to turn her plump self around to see the long figure of that highly efficient financier stretched out in its black-and-white-checked tennis-flannel nightgown, sleeping the sleep of the model citizen and father.

No, Mother had only reached one of those occasional signboards in life that say "Fagged! Relax! Let up! Nothing doing!" She was suffering from a slight attack of mental and spiritual *ennui,* which is a polite way of saying that her digestion was getting sluggish. She was fifty-two, not exactly senile, but certainly not as gay as, say, *twenty*-two.

Just then the connoisseur of mortgages rolled over heavily like a sleepy porpoise and muttered something that sounded like "Ain oo cum bed?"

Fifty-two! she went on thinking, and she had never had a day to herself to do just as she liked. From that day, twenty-five years ago, when the nurse laid the red and colicky Bob in her arms, her time had belonged to others. In memory she could see Henry's white, drawn face as he knelt by her bed and said:

"Molly, you'll never, *never* have to go through this again."

But she had! Oh land, yes! Bob was twenty-five, Katherine was twenty-two, Marcia twenty-one, Eleanor sixteen, and Junior eleven — all healthy, good-looking, fun-loving and thoughtless. She had been a slave to them, of course. She ought to know it by this time, every one had told her so.

But it wasn't just the family. There was the

church — and the club — and the Library Board. Oh, she was hemmed in on all sides! Always, every one thought, Mrs. Mason would do this and that and the other thing. Why did people think she could attend to so many duties? She was just an *easy mark!* This week, for instance: this was Monday night; to-morrow afternoon she was to lead the missionary meeting; to-morrow night the Marstons were coming to play Somerset. They came every Tuesday night. She and John Marston would bid wildly against Sarah Marston's and Henry's slower playing, and Henry and Sarah would probably win. Henry's bidding was like his banking — calm, studied, conservative. Then she would serve sandwiches and fruit salad and coffee. Why did she rack her brain to think of dainty new things to feed them every Tuesday night, just to hear them say, "Lordy, Molly, your things melt in the mouth!"

Wednesday, the Woman's Club was to meet with her, and besides entertaining she had to get her paper into better shape to read. It had been Mrs. Hayes's date, but she couldn't have them — or didn't want them — and of course they had asked to come to Mrs. Mason's. Well, being an easy mark, *she* could put all the chairs away afterward and pick up the ballots strewn around.

Wednesday night was the church supper. Why had *she* baked the beans and made the coffee for *years?* Thursday afternoon the Library Board must meet, and Thursday night Junior's Sunday school class was to have a party in the basement of the church. She must go whether she felt like it or not, and help with the refreshments and play "Going to Jerusalem" until she was all out of breath and — oh, *why* did she have to keep on doing so many things for others? It was as though she had no personality. Never a day to herself to do just as she liked!

Tired and cross, she brushed her hair spitefully. Then her eyes fell upon a motto-calendar, silver framed, on the dresser. In gay red letters it flaunted itself:

> ... Know ye not
> Who would be free themselves must strike the blow?
> Byron, "Childe Harold."

Could a message be more personal? Underneath the calendar the detested lower plate of teeth reposed in a little Japanese dish which was their nightly bed. She picked them up and held them distastefully in her hand, so uncannily human, so blatantly artificial. And suddenly, born of rebellious mood and childish

14

desire, was brought forth a plan.

She rose from her chair and undressed. Then she knelt by the side of the bed and said her prayer, a little rambling, vague complaint: "Oh, Lord; I'm so tired of the same things — and everybody expects so much of me — and there are so many things to do — and it won't be just a lie — if You know all about it — and why I did it — Amen."

And maybe, to the Good One who heard her, she seemed only a very fat little girl with a thin little pigtail hanging down her back.

Mother rose stiffly from her knees, snapped out the lights, and lay down beside the president of the First National Bank, who mumbled drowsily, "Hut time ist?"

At the breakfast table, Mother casually announced, as though she were accustomed to these gay little jaunts, that she was taking the nine-twenty train for Capitol City. It was like a hand grenade in their midst.

"*You*, Mother?" . . . "Why" . . . "What for?" . . . "You can't! It's Missionary Day!" came the shrapnel return.

"She's going to see Doctor Reeve about her plate." Father had been previously informed, it seemed.

"Her plate?" . . . "What plate?" . . . "Card plate?" . . . "Haviland plate?" . . . "Home plate?" Every one giggled. The Great

American Family thoroughly appreciates its own wit.

"Sh!" Marcia tapped her own pretty mouth.

"The hours I've spent with Doctor Reeve
Are but a china set to me —
I count them over, every one apart,
My crockery! My crockery!"

They all laughed hilariously, all but Mother. They were not cruel, not even impertinent. But they were intensely fun-loving, a trait inherited from Mother herself. Strangely enough, humor, Mother's faithful partner for fifty-two years, had suddenly turned tail and fled, leaving only its lifeless mask which she surveyed in tragic dignity. Very well, let them make fun of her if they so wished.

There was some discussion as to which one should take Mother to the train. She settled it herself; there was a reason why she chose to walk. On analysis, she would have discovered that this reason was not to interrupt the new sensation of feeling sorry for herself.

She would have liked to make the trip to the station in mournful solitude, but Henry must have been watching for her, for he grabbed his hat and came running down the bank steps as she passed.

"Have you got plenty of blank checks?" he

wanted to know.

All the way down Main Street Henry chatted sociably. When the train whistled in he said, "Well, Mother, we'll meet you to-night on the five-fifty" — and kissed her. In ordinary times a tender kiss from any member of her family had the effect of melting Mother into a substance resembling putty; but to-day she had no more feeling for her tribe than the cement platform on which she stood.

As she settled herself in the car, Henry came to the window and said something. The train was starting and she couldn't hear. So he shouted it: "You sure you got plenty of blank checks?"

"Yes, yes!"

She nodded irritably as though he had said something insulting.

At Capitol City Mother went immediately to the Delevan — rather timidly, to be sure, for Father had always been with her when they registered.

"Single rooms, three, four and five dollars," said the jaunty clerk.

"Five dollars," said Mother boldly, as befitted the wife of Henry Y. Mason.

There was a little time to shop before lunch, so she walked over to Sterling's and bought one nightgown, one kimono, and one pair of soft slippers. After lunch she sent a telegram to Henry:

Find lots to be done. Home Friday night.

Well, she had cut loose, burned her bridges! For three days she would escape that long list of energy-killing things. She would think of no one but herself, do nothing but what she wished to do.

In the afternoon she sauntered past the movie theaters, reading the billboards. To the hurrying passer-by she was only a heavily-built, motherly-looking person in a gray voile dress and small gray and black hat. In reality she was Freedom-from-Her-Mountain-Height.

In the theater, as she took nibbles from a box of candy and listened to the orchestra, if any thought of the missionary meeting with its lesson on "Our Work Among the Burmese Women" came to her, it was in pity for the feminine population of Burma who knew not the rapture of complete liberty.

She laughed delightedly and wept frankly over the joys and sorrows of the popular star, who whisked energetically through seven reels.

Out of the theater again, she loitered by the plate glass windows of the big stores, went in and out as fancy dictated, and bought a few things — always for herself.

When she returned to the Delevan there was a long-distance call for her. It was Henry: "This you, Mother? Say, I could just as well come down on the night train and stay with you until you're all through your work."

"Oh, no, no," she assured him. "I'm perfectly all right. I'm *fine*. I wouldn't *think* of it."

"You got plenty of blank checks?"

"Yes, *yes!*" Mother was smiling into the transmitter. Her grouch was as much a thing of the past as the battle of Gettysburg.

At dinner she ordered food for the first time in her life without running her finger up and down the price column. After resting a while in complete comfort, she sallied forth again. A famous tenor was singing at the Auditorium. His "Mother Machree" gave her a momentary twinge of conscience-itis, but she quickly recovered. Even the Mother Machree of the song may have had one wild fling some time in her life.

There were two more whole days of complete emancipation. Club afternoon, when she should have read her paper on "Pottery — Ancient and Modern," she was attending "The Vampire." She had always wondered just what that particular blood-sucking animal was like, and she was finding out.

When she left the theater it was sprinkling, and by dinner time there was a downpour. But after dining she went through the storm to a theater where a merry troupe demonstrated how one may effectively kick and sing at the same time. *Now,* Mother thought, as she watched the twinkling heels, the women were clearing up that awful mess of church-supper dishes and wondering how it happened they had fallen short of chicken and had three times as many noodles as they needed. Thank her stars, *she* had escaped it!

On Thursday she took a long street car ride, read comfortably in her room, went to two movies, and attended an art exhibit. The Library Board was meeting at home, of course, and listening half the afternoon to the Reverend Mr. Patterson tell how he started a library at Beaver Junction forty years ago. Then Junior's class was cavorting through those never-ending games of "Tin-Tin-Come-In" and "Beast-Bird-Fish-or-Fowl." Well, thank fortune, some other mother was getting a dose of assisting Miss Jenkins with her irrepressibles.

Friday morning Mother went up to Doctor Reeve's office. Friday afternoon she went home. On the train she reviewed her pleasurable three days. She had solved the problem. Life need never again become too strenuous. How simple it all was. The foolish part was that she had never thought of the plan before. She had only to slip away in peace and solitude whenever a week piled up with duties as the past one had. Good sense told her that she would not do it often, but it would always lie there before her — the way of beatific escape.

The train was rumbling through the cut in the Bluffs now, where lay the ghosts of many dead picnics, rounding the curve toward the water tank, slowing at the familiar station. There they were, Henry and Marcia and Eleanor — assembled as if they were about to greet the President of the United States. Junior, hanging by one arm and leg from a telephone pole, was waving his cap like a friendly orang-outang.

They kissed her rapturously — the girls and Junior. Henry's kiss, while resembling less a combustion, was frankly tender.

"Your dental work hurt you, Mother?"

"Oh, not a great deal." She was cheerfully brave.

They hung about her, all talking at once as they moved in a tight little bunch toward the car.

"Kathie's got two girls home from the University for over Sunday," they were telling her. "We had Tillie bake a cake and make mayonnaise and dress chickens for dinner to-night, but Papa wouldn't let her fry 'em — wants you to do it. And, Mamma, you've got to lead Missionary Meeting next Tuesday, Mrs. Fat Perkins said to tell you. They didn't have it last Tuesday."

"And to-night's paper said in the club notes that Mrs. Mason would read her paper on dishes, or kettles, or something like that next Wednesday."

"Oh, Muz!" It was Junior jumping back-ward in front of them and shouting. "We didn't have our party — Miss Jenkins said you'd be back to help next Thursday. Ain't that dandy?"

"They put off the library meeting till you got home, too."

"Did they?" A tidal wave of chuckles was forming somewhere in Mother's stout interior. "Did they by any possible chance have the church supper?"

"No, they never," they were all answering. "It was so rainy, and they 'phoned around, and they said anyway you weren't here to do the beans and coffee. It's next Wednesday."

"Oh, I guess you didn't miss much, Molly." Henry gave her substantial arm a friendly squeeze and beamed down at her. "The Mar-stons are coming tonight."

The tidal wave rolled in — or up. Mother was laughing hysterically. Humor, her faithful partner for fifty-two years, had returned from his mysterious vacation, and with the rest of the family had met Mother at the station.

Mother sat in front of her Circassian walnut dressing table. It was eleven o'clock. She had just come upstairs after setting the bread. She removed the heavy gray braid, laid it on the dresser and let down her scant hair. Then she took from her mouth the detested thing — so luridly red, so ghastly white — and surveyed it critically to see whether there remained a visible trace of the minute defect that Doctor Reeve's assistant in four minutes had ground down in his laboratory.

As she laid the plate in its Japanese dish, her eyes fell upon the silver-framed calendar. The old date was now ancient history. Mother removed the card and slipped the new page into place. In black and gilt it grinned impishly at her:

> Freedom is only in the Land of Dreams.
> Schiller.

Mother got into her nightgown and knelt by the bed to say her prayer. It was neither vague and wandering, nor was it a complaint. It was a concise little expression of gratitude, direct and sincere: "Dear Lord: I always felt that You must have a humorous side and now I am sure of it. The joke's on me. And, Lord, I'll be good and never be cross again about doing all the little everyday things for the folks about me. Amen."

Then she rose, snapped off the lights and lay down beside the president of the First National Bank, who mumbled sleepily, "Hut time ist?"

CHAPTER II

INTRODUCING THE FAMILY

Mother having been introduced, it would be well to get a glimpse of the other members of the Mason household — a "close-up" of each, as it were.

Mother herself, standing on that plateau of life where one looks both hopefully forward and longingly back, felt that life had been very gracious to her. It had brought her health, happiness, and Henry — and sometimes, in a spasm of loyal devotion, she decided that the greatest of these was Henry.

For thirty-five years Henry Mason had given his time, his thought, his every waking moment to building up the First National Bank of Springtown. He was not only a part of the bank, he *was* the bank. He knew every man in the community, his financial rating, his capabilities, his shortcomings, his life history.

The country banker is an entirely different species from your city banker. The city banker may hold his hand on the pulse of the nation's financial ebb and flow, but your country banker lives close to the hearts of the people. He is the financial pastor of his flock. "Better slow up, Jim," he will say; "you're running bigger grocery bills than a family of your size ought to have." And sometimes Jim doesn't like it, says the old man better mind his own business; but it is noticeable that he takes the advice to heart.

The country banker is also lawyer, judge, physician. In his little back office, thick with smoke, spattered with gaudy calendars and farm-sale bills, he advises his patrons when to sell hogs and when to marry, when to buy bunches of yearlings and when to have their appendixes removed. He carries a burden of confidences that is far from being merely financial, a burden of greater proportions than the minister's.

Father was not a great church worker. His voice was never raised in the congregation; but not every one who saith Lord, Lord, shall enter into the kingdom. His religion was a very simple thing. He made no public demonstration of it, but he did a great many things unto the "least of these." He saw that more than one load of wood and sack of potatoes found their way to tumble-down back doors. He sent lame Annie Bassert to business school.

When Lizzie Beadle came into the bank and wanted a loan to take her old mother to the sanitarium, Father refused the loan at the bank window because there was no security; but he called Lizzie into the back office and made out his personal check to her. Business was business at the grated window, but the back office was his own.

Once the influential members of the community wanted to send Father to the legislature. It pleased him immensely, but he would have given his right hand rather than let on how gratified was his pride. He thought it all over and then, "Thank you, boys," he said; "guess I'd better just stay here and saw wood."

He was a son of the soil, was Henry Mason. He had come from good old farmer stock. One of his earliest recollections was lying flat on the bottom of a prairie schooner and watching the coarse wild grass billow away from the big wooden wheels.

That very characteristic, love of the soil, was his greatest asset as a country banker. The members of the bank force had a joke among themselves concerning this. It was about farm sales. That is another phase of country banking of which your city banker lives in dark and fathomless ignorance. In the country communities of the great Mid-West, the winter and early spring dispersion sales draw vast crowds of buyers to the various farms. To each sale goes the farmer's banker to set up a miniature place in which to do banking business for the day. It is usually the cashier or an assistant who is listed for the work, seldom the older president, for the work is dirty, the whole day hard.

Father, however, reveled in the earth smells, the tramping stock, the call of the auctioneer, the noon-day lunch in the farmyard. On the morning of a sale day he talked of nothing else. He asked each customer as soon as he stepped inside the bank if he intended going. He walked around restlessly, looking out of the big windows at the sky, wondering what the weather would be.

D. T. Smith, the cashier, and Bob Mason, and the other two boys would all wink at each other. Bob might say, "Gee, I certainly hate to go out in this wind." Father always fell for it. "Wind? My golly, Son, that's just a little breeze."

"Don't feel like going yourself, do you, Father?"

And Father, trying not to answer too hastily that he'd just as soon go if Bob didn't want to, could scarcely get away fast enough to the locker, where he kept an old moth-eaten Galloway coat, an equally dilapidated cap, and a pair of hip boots. He would leave for the sale as happy as a little boy going on a fishing trip, and the minute the door closed the force would laugh and chuckle at the joke before settling down to the cleaner indoor work of the day.

To Mother a farm sale was always a trial. In addition to the mud-spattered condition in which Father often returned, he always bought something, some outlandish worn-out thing for which they had no possible use.

"Nobody bid on it," Father would explain apologetically, as though the statement vindicated him.

As some men collect Sir Joshua Reynolds and Corots, so Father collected odds and ends from the farm sales. Once he bought a broken grindstone, and one time a sickly calf, and once a pair of collapsible bedsprings that collapsed perfectly but failed to have any other virtue.

"He's missed his calling," Marcia would say pertly before him. "He's really by nature and inclination a junk dealer, you know."

"He can't help it, poor dear!" Katherine would add. "Some men can't resist gambling, but Father can't resist bidding on old trash."

"I'm saving them for your wedding presents, Kathie," Father would retort good-naturedly, which lately had the effect of bringing a shell-pink ripple of color to

Katherine's smooth cheek.

Katherine was the eldest Mason daughter, serious-eyed, lithe and lovely — and just graduated from the State University. In the bosom of her family Katherine held the self-appointed office of Head Critic. With zeal and finesse she engaged in constant attempts to manage the activities of the other Masons. Their manners, their grammar, their very opinions on art, literature, and music were supervised by the eldest daughter and sister. To be sure, results were far from satisfactory to the ardent critic; the Masons, individually and collectively being of a too independent disposition to follow dictation, sheeplike. At Katherine's unceasing efforts to bring them all up to certain standards of propriety, they merely shrugged their shoulders and went blithely on their respective ways. They loved her, but they did not obey her.

Marcia, the second daughter, was only a year younger than Katherine and had completed her Junior year at the University. There is in this world an occasional gay, care-free person who seems to be wafted not only to the skies but through life itself on flowery beds of ease. Such a *rara avis* was Marcia. While Katherine's nature was of a sweet seriousness and given to earnest study, Marcia's was neither of these.

If she was serious, she concealed it admirably. Her studying was usually a very hasty procedure, conducted on the way down a corridor to her recitation room. She had a flour-sieve mind, warranted to hold a great deal of information for at least twenty minutes.

"I always volunteer during the first part of the recitation while the going's good," she brazenly told at home, "then my silence isn't so conspicuous when the road gets rough."

Things seemed to come Marcia's way.

"I was born under a lucky star," she often told the family. And the family almost believed it.

In appearance she was undeniably lovely, and, as one of her aunts said, "as likable as she was lookable." No one could say she was lazy about the house. She simply made a wise and far-sighted choice of household tasks. Soon after she had enthusiastically offered to shell the peas, it became apparent to the other girls that the pea-shelling operation carried on under the breeze-swept grape arbor was greatly preferable to doing the dishes in the hot kitchen or making countless beds.

"Marcia certainly has the happy faculty of slipping through life easily," Mother would sometimes say in exasperation to Father.

"Well, Mother, I don't know any one in the family that makes more friends," Father would remind her.

Which brings us to Father and Mother Mason's attitude toward and about their children. For twenty-six years they had argued over them, but always when they were alone. Toward the children they presented a solid front. If Mother chose to reprove, Father either assisted at the ceremony or kept silent. And *vice versa*. It is a fine old policy. It has been effective since the days of Abraham and Sarah.

When they were alone, however, they argued it out. And the strange part is that neither one always took the same side. If Mother found fault with some characteristic of her offspring, Father immediately made excuses for it. If Father offered the complaint, Mother flew to her child's defense like a mother bear.

In this instance Father was right about Marcia's friends. Everybody liked her, the teachers and old people and children, and Hod Beeson, who brought the coal, and Lizzie Beadle, the town dressmaker.

When Marcia went away to school, it was as though a great deal of the sunshine of the Mason home had gone with her. When she returned for vacations, everything and every one, from the piano to Tillie, seemed to brighten at her coming. After all, the old world needs more of them — these people who turn to joyousness as the tides run to meet the moon.

Each time Marcia came home she had new tales to tell. And Father and Mother, who came to reprove, remained to laugh.

"Say, folks," she would begin, "I had to write a thesis on some form of lower animal life for old Prof. Briggs in zoölogy class, and what I know about zoölogy you could put in a *spoon*. So I wrote about a starfish — sort of from the fiction standpoint — and they told me old Prof. Briggs laughed till he nearly cried over the joys and sorrows of that little echinoderm — I *guess* it's an echinoderm. I got a grade of excellent, and all I know about a starfish to this *day* is that it has five points and *wiggles*."

"You can't go through life side-stepping that way, my girl," Father sermonized after he had suppressed a chuckle. "One of these days you'll bump up against something mighty serious and wish you'd applied yourself."

"Don't preach, Father!" Marcia rubbed a pink and white cheek against Father's graying hair. "When that time comes I'll be like Sentimental Tommy — I'll find a way." And softhearted old Father hoped it was true.

No one ever spoke of Eleanor, the sixteen-year-old daughter, as being pretty. By the side of Katherine's Madonnalike sweetness and

Marcia's loveliness, Eleanor was rather plain, but she was merry hearted, and a merry heart maketh a cheerful countenance.

Instead of being the possessor of large, luminous eyes like the other girls, she had smaller, twinkling ones, like Mother's. Most people laugh first with their mouths, but when anything pleased Eleanor, which was about four hundred times a day, there came a little crinkling at the corner of her lids so that her eyes seemed to laugh before their mirth communicated itself to her generous mouth.

Of the three girls she had always been the most hoydenish. Many an old lady in Springtown could testify to having been nearly frightened out of her wits at the diabolical speed with which Eleanor Mason rode a bicycle. She could hold her own in baseball, and she was the star guard of the high school basketball team.

Clothes she considered mere articles of apparel, worn from the necessity of being decently covered. It was sometimes recalled in the family that once, to give Eleanor more pride in her clothes, Mother had sent her to Lizzie Beadle, with two nice pieces of serge and the instructions to plan both dresses herself. On the way Eleanor had encountered Junior and a crowd of neighborhood boys, who wanted her to pitch for them. She had rushed up to the house of the Beadle lady, thrust the bundle in the door and called out, "Make 'em just alike, Miss Beadle," and taken herself off to the more glowing pleasures of the Mason cow pasture.

Boys she looked upon simply as the male of the species, somewhat to be envied for having been endowed by the gods with stronger right arms and an apparent aptitude for mathematics, denied to Eleanor herself.

To be sure, there was a Land of Romance, but it was peopled with no one she had really ever seen. The Prince and the Sleeping Beauty were there, and Laurie and Amy from the pages of *Little Women*, and Babbie and the little minister. If there occasionally walked some one in the shadowy forest that seemed to belong to her, alone, he was too far away and vague to take on any semblance of reality.

Junior was eleven. The statement is significant.

There are a few peevish people in the world who believe that all eleven-year-old boys ought to be hung. Others, less irritable, think that gently chloroforming them would seem more humane. A great many good-natured folks contend that incarceration for a couple of years would prove the best way to dispose of them.

Just how Springtown was divided in regard

to Junior and his crowd of cronies depended largely upon the amiability of its citizens. But practically every one looked upon that crowd as he looked upon other pests: rust, sparrows, moth millers, and potato bugs. As the boys came out of school tearing wildly down the street with Apache yells, more than one staid citizen had been seen to cross the road hurriedly as one would get out of the way of fire engines, or molten lava rolling down from Vesuvius.

There were a dozen or more boys in the crowd, but the ringleaders were Runt Perkins, Shorty Marston, and Junior Mason, and the only similarity between charity and Junior was that the greatest of these was Junior.

At home, by the united efforts of the other members of the Mason family, he was kept subdued into something resembling civilized man. Mother ruled him with a firm hand but an understanding heart. The girls made strenuous efforts to assist in his upbringing, but their gratuitous services were not kindly looked upon by the young man, who believed it constituted mere butting-in.

Katherine it was who took upon herself the complete charge of his speech. Not an insignificant "have went" nor an infinitesimal "I seen" ever escaped the keen ears of his eldest sister, who immediately corrected him.

Mother sometimes thought Katherine a little severe when, in the interest of proper speaking, she could stop him in the midst of an exciting account of a home-run. There were times, thought Mother, when the spirit of the thing was so much more important than the flesh in which it was clothed.

For arithmetic Junior showed such an aptitude that Father was wont to say encouragingly, "You'll be working in the bank one of these days, Son." At which "Son" would glow with a legitimate pride that quickly faded before the sight of a certain dull red book entitled *Working Lessons in English Grammar.* Katherine labored patiently many an evening to assist in bringing Junior and the contents of this particular volume somewhere within hailing distance of each other. Painstakingly she would go over the ground with him in preparation for his lessons, to be met with a situation something like this:

"Now we're ready. Read the first sentence, Junior."

And Junior would earnestly and enthusiastically sing-song: " 'He *took* his *coat* down *from* the *nail* with*out a word* of *warn*ing.' "

"What's the subject, Junior? Now think!"

"Coat," Junior would answer promptly. Then, seeing Katherine's grieved look, he would change quickly to "Nail." And when the look deepened to disgust he would grow wild and begin guessing frantically: "Warning? Took? From?"

Of the three girls Eleanor was his best friend. Rather boyish herself, she was still not so far removed from the glamour of ball games in the back pasture, the trapping of gophers, and circuses in the barn, but that the two held many things in common.

It was Marcia who was his arch enemy. Not that she committed any serious offenses. It was her attitude that exasperated him. She had a trick of perpetrating a lazy little smile on his every act, a smile that was of a surpassing superiority. And she had a way of always jumping at the conclusion that he was dirty. "Go *wash* your *hands!*" was her sisterly greeting whenever he approached. She used it as consistently toward him as she used "How do you do?" to other people. Junior would jump into a heated argument over his perfect cleanliness, a discussion that consumed more time than an entire bath would have taken.

With catalogue-like completeness this finishes the list of the Mason family members who were still at home, for Bob and his young wife, Mabel, and the new baby girl who had recently arrived, lived two blocks away. Like a supplement to the register, however, there still remains Tillie who was as much a part of the household as Father or the kitchen sink.

Tillie Horn — her church letter and bank book said Matilda Horn — had lived in the Mason household for eighteen years. Accordingly to present-day standards her position there was hard to define. Guest? No. Mother silently put a check on the kitchen clock shelf every Saturday morning, and Tillie as surreptitiously removed it sometime during the day. It was one of Tillie's forty odd characteristics that she disliked to speak of her wages. Several times in the eighteen years, as the H. C. of L. thrust itself with nightmare ferocity on an unwary world, the amount on the check had been voluntarily raised by Mother, to which Tillie had made grateful and appreciative response, "Wha'd you do that silly thing for?"

Domestic servant? The day the new doctor's wife returned Mother's call, she asked affably, "Do you find your servant satisfactory?" As smooth as lubricating oil, Mother answered, "I have none. My old friend Miss Horn lives with us and helps me." Then she called pleasantly, "Come in, Tillie, and meet Mrs. Cummings." Which of course was not at all according to Hoyle. But then Mother did not do things by footrules and yardsticks. She did them by friendly instinct. And when you stop to think about it, that is a fairly good definition of a lady and a Christian.

No, Tillie was not a servant. For those eighteen years she had alternately worked like a Trojan or "slicked up" and gone comfortably to Mite Societies and Missionary Meetings with Mother.

The two had known each other years before in the more or less pleasant intimacy of a cross-roads schoolhouse, where Tillie's education had abruptly ceased. Mother had gone away to school, taught, been married, and was in the midst of the triple-ringed circus act of trying to raise three babies at once when Tillie dropped in one day between trains to call upon her. That call had lasted eighteen years, broken only by two intervals.

In appearance Tillie was all that any enterprising movie director could desire. She was tall, angular, homely. Her long neck, rising from the habitually worn, dull gray kitchen dress, was slightly crooked, like a Hubbard squash's. Hair, to Tillie, meant nothing by way of being a woman's crowning glory. It was merely, as the dictionary so ably states, small horny, fibrous tubes with bulbous roots, growing out of the skins of mammals; and it was meant to be combed down as flat as possible and held in place with countless wire hairpins. Her eyes were small and nondescript in color, her mouth and nose large, and her teeth of a glaring china-white falseness. Altogether, it was a lucky thing for Tillie that while man looketh on the outward appearance the Lord looketh on the heart. For Tillie's heart was as good as gold, and was buried under just about the same proportion of crusty exterior as the yellow metal under the earth.

Tillie's sense of humor, or lack of it, was not an understandable thing to the fun-loving Masons. The ancient author who copyrighted most of the wise sayings of the world once stated that there was a time to weep and a time to laugh. Tillie seemed never to know when that time was. Over things that the whole family shouted about, she maintained a dignified and critical silence. On the other hand, she would occasionally break out into a high, weird, hen-like cackle over the most trivial thing imaginable. If the Masons laughed then, it was not at the trifling joke but because Tillie herself was so odd.

"My stars! Listen to Tillie!" one of the girls would say. "I'll bet a nickel she's just found out it's Thursday morning instead of Friday."

"Or picked up the egg beater instead of the potato masher," another would guess.

No, in spite of the long association with a family whose chief delight in life was the foolish little fun extracted by the way, Tillie's sense of humor was almost negligible. And it is easier for the keeper of five cinnamon bears to control his charges without chains and a prodding pole, than it is for any member of a household that contains five hilarious young people to exist comfortably with them, minus a highly developed sense of humor.

A buffer being any contrivance that serves to deaden the concussion caused by the impact of two bodies, it became apparent, when the children were growing up, that such an apparatus was needed between them and Tillie. And with that clear perception with which some people see their duty, Mother very early discovered that she, herself, must be that device. During all these years she had stood between her noisy, merry brood and this old friend, whose ideas of life were invoiced in terms of sweeping and scrubbing.

With that capacity for sinking herself in another's personality, Mother could clearly see both sides of a situation, and as for the diplomatic handling of it, she was an able ambassador to the Court of the Kitchen. So she had tactfully handled each *affaire d'honneur* from the days when Bob's kites littered up the back porch, through the period of the girls messing around with dough, down to Junior's high jinks. Firmly had she made a stand for Tillie's right to have certain hours in the day to herself, and staunchly had she defended the children's legitimate desires for picnic lunches and other childish necessities. Yes, Mother certainly deadened the concussion caused by the impact of two bodies.

The two intervals in which Tillie had not worked for the Masons were occasions when she had become vaguely dissatisfied and gone away to live permanently with her own relatives. The first time, after being gone two months, she wrote Mother and asked if she might come back, that she couldn't abide her sister's husband and would die happy if she could only put him on her mop stick and scrub the kitchen floor with him.

The other time she had gone to a cousin's, returning in three weeks with the information that her cousin's daughters both had beaus, and they made her sick with what she chose to call their "lally-gagging" around. Aversion to the display of sentiment being another of Tillie's characteristics, no one was surprised.

If she ever had a romance of her own, no one knew of it. It was often recalled in the family that Hod Beeson, erstwhile a drayman by profession and a widower by Providence, had once come to the back door on a Sunday night, dressed in his best. To the unsuspecting Tillie who opened the door this smiling Lochinvar had ventured jauntily, "It's a nice evening, Miss Horn." But, unlike Ellen of

Netherby Hall, Tillie had snapped out, "Maybe so. I ain't noticed it," and peremptorily shut the door.

With this intimate view of the Mason family whose members form the cast of characters — the stage the comfortable, commodious home of a middle-west country banker — the little plays are ready. And let only those of you who can sense the fun and tragedy in the everyday ups-and-downs of the ordinary American family, the kind of folks that live next door to you and me — read on.

CHAPTER III

KATHERINE ENTERTAINS

In the week that followed Mother's return from Capitol City, she slipped back into the old routine with doubled energy, attending cheerfully all the meetings which she so gullibly believed she had missed in her dash for liberty. But through it all one great event stood out with arc light brilliancy: that on Sunday the family was to entertain company.

Entertaining company in itself was nothing unusual, the Sundays in which it occurred probably outnumbering those in which the family ate alone. But on this coming June Sunday it was the guest-to-be, himself, who was out of the ordinary.

Specifically, he was to be Katherine's company, but the family had been cautioned by Mother that they were by no manner of means to refer to him as Katherine's individual acquisition.

The coming guest, Keith Baldridge, was assistant professor of history in Katherine's

Alma Mater. He was thirty-two and unmarried. No, he was not Katherine's fiancé — Katherine's manner dared any one to suggest it. As a matter of fact, their friendship was at that very delicate stage where the least breath might shrivel the emerging chrysalis, or blow it into a gorgeous-winged creature of Love.

In the meantime, it was going to be an awful strain on the family to have him come. Mother was already feeling the effects of Katherine's attempts to make over the entire family in the four days intervening before his arrival.

"How long's Bald Head goin' to stay?" Junior wanted to know at the supper table in the middle of the week.

"There he goes, Mamma," Katherine said plaintively. "Can't you keep him from saying those horrid things?"

"My son," Father addressed him from the head of the table, "have you ever heard of the children in the Bible who were eaten by bears when they said, 'Go up, thou bald head'?" Junior grinned appreciatively, realizing he was not being very violently reproved.

"If you could just know, Mamma, how different the Baldridge home is from ours!" Katherine was in the kitchen now, assisting Mother and Tillie. "Our family is so talkative and noisy, and laughs over every little silly thing, and there's is so much *confusion*. Why, at their dinners — beside Professor Baldridge there's just his father and an aunt, both *so* aristocratic — at their dinners it's so quiet and the conversation is so *enlightening* — about Rodin, and — and Wagner — and, oh, maybe Milton's "Il Penseroso" — you know what I mean — so much more *refined*."

At that word, Mother had an unholy desire to recall to the polished, critical girl before her the days when she used to hang, head downward, from the apple tree, her abbreviated skirts obediently following the direction of her head. But she forbore. Mothers are like that.

"And I wish you could *see* their house. It's not as big as ours, and really no nicer, but, oh! the *atmosphere!* The hangings are gray or mauve or dark purple — and they keep the shades down so much lower than ours — so it's peaceful, you know, like twilight all the time."

"My stars! Ain't that a gloomy way to live, and unhealthy, too, I must say." It was Tillie speaking acridly with the familiarity which comes from having braided a little girl's hair and officiated at the coming out party of her first tooth.

"And pictures!" Katherine went on, ignoring Tillie's disgusted remark. "Why, folks, in one room there's just *one*, a dull dim, old wood scene, and so *artistic*. You can imagine how Papa's bank calendar in our dining room just makes me *sick*. And they have a Japanese servant. You never hear him coming, but suddenly he's right there at your elbow, so quiet and —"

"My good land! How spooky!"

"Oh, Tillie, *no!* It's the most exquisite service you ever saw — to have him gliding in and out and anticipating your every wish."

"Well, Kathie, I'll wait table for you, and glad to, but I ain't goin' to do no slippin' around like that heathen, as if I was at a spiritual séance, I can promise you that."

"Thank you, Tillie, and, Tillie, when you pass things to him, please don't say anything to him, he's so used to that unobtrusive kind of being waited on — and he's so quiet and reserved himself."

"Well, if I had a glum man like that, I'd mop the floor with him." Tillie was always going to mop the floor with some one.

At that, Katherine left the kitchen with dignity, which gave Tillie a chance to say, "Ain't she the beatenest! I declare, she riles me so this week!" To which Mother replied, "Don't be too hard on her, Tillie. It's exasperating,

48

I know; but she's nervous. Sakes alive! Don't I remember to this day just how I felt sitting around in a new lavender lawn dress thinking Henry might come. He had a pair of spotted ponies, and went driving furiously past our farm for three different evenings before he had the courage to stop." And Mother laughed at the recollection.

It was a characteristic of Mother's — this being able to project herself into another's personality. In the days that followed she seemed to live a Jekyll-Hyde existence. She was her own exasperated self because of Katherine's constant haranguing about the way things ought to be, and she was Katherine, sensitive, easily affected, standing quiveringly in the wings of the stage at the Great Play — waiting for her cue.

Because of this trait, Mother had known, to her finger tips, the griefs and joys of each member of her family — how Father felt the year bank deposits dropped forty-five per cent, how Junior felt when he made the grammar Nine. Some call it sympathy. Others call it discernment. In reality, it is the concentrated essence of all the mother wisdom of the ages.

Mother was worried, too. She had never seen Keith Baldridge, and numerous questions of doubt filled her mind. What manner of man was this that lived in a house of perpetual twilight?

The family managed to live through Thursday, Friday, and Saturday. The word *Sunday* seemed to have a portentous meaning, as though it were the day set apart for a cyclone, or something dreadful was to happen to the sun.

Professor Baldridge was coming in his car sometime in the morning. He had to leave in the afternoon, as he was to go around by Miles City to get his aunt, who was visiting there, and take her home. In truth, that had been his excuse for coming at all.

It came — *Sunday*. To the Mason family it was "Der Tag." It proved to be a still, hot morning, full of humidity and the buzzing and bumbling of insects.

At the breakfast table Katherine gave the last of her multitudinous directions. "Mamma, I wish you'd *muzzle* Junior. Make him promise not to *open* his head."

"My child" — Mother's tone signified that it was making its last patient stand — "Junior shall be the pink of propriety, I assure you; but not for the President of the United States would I frighten one of my children into silence."

Simultaneously, Marcia and Eleanor hooted. "Imagine anybody being able to frighten Junior into silence!" was their combined exclamation.

After breakfast, Katherine, like General Pershing, reviewed her troops, the house and the grounds. From vestibule to back porch, through the big reception hall, library, living-room, sun-parlor, everything was immaculate. There was not a flicker of dust in the house. There was not a stick or dead leaf on the lawn.

Marcia, Eleanor, and Junior all trooped off to Sunday school and Father followed later to church, but Mother and Tillie stood by the guns, preparing ammunition in the form of salad and chicken. Katherine, who by this time was in such a palpitating state of heart that she could not assist intelligently at anything, went upstairs to dress.

When she had finished — she decided on white after having had on a pink and a pale green — she sat down on her cedar chest, with eyes glued on the driveway. For some time she sat there, starting up at the sound of every car. Then she saw some one turning in at the front walk. He was short and slightly stooped. He carried a cane, but seemed to hobble along without using it. He wore store clothes too large for him and a black, wide-brimmed felt hat over his white hair. *It was Grandpa,* Grandpa Warner, who lived with another

51

daughter on his old home farm, and had evidently come to surprise Mother's family.

Katherine started up with a cry. Not that! Oh, not Grandpa *to-day!* It was too cruel! Why, Grandpa monopolized conversation with his reminiscences, and at the table he did unspeakable things with his knife.

The good fairy which is called Memory reminded Katherine of the days when she had slipped her hand into Grandpa's and gone skipping along with him through dewy, honey-sweet clover to drive the cows down to the lower pasture; days when she had snuggled down by him in the old homemade sleigh and been whirled through an elfland of snow-covered trees and ice-locked rivulets; days that seemed then to embody to her all the happiness that time could hold. But she turned coldly away from the wistful fairy, and looked bitterly out upon a day that was unconditionally spoiled.

Carrying herself reluctantly downstairs, she perfunctorily greeted the old man. Mother, the happy moisture in her eyes, was making a great fuss over him. Temporarily she had forgotten that such a personage as Keith Baldridge existed.

Back in a few moments to her room, Katherine continued her watchful waiting.

A car turned in at the driveway, a long,

low, gray car and Keith Baldridge, in ulster and auto cap, stepped out. At the sight of the figure that was almost never out of her mind, she dropped on her knees by the cedar chest and covered her face with her hands, as though the vision blinded her. And those who think her only ridiculously sentimental do not understand how the heart of a girl goes timidly down the Great White Road to meet its mate.

As for Mother, when Keith Baldridge grasped her hand, her own heart dropped from something like ninety beats to its normal seventy-two. He was big and athletic-looking, and under well-modeled brows shone gray-blue eyes that were unmistakably frank and kind. With that God-given intuition of Mother's she knew that he was *clean* — clean in mind and soul and body. And quite suddenly she wanted him for her girl, wanted him as ardently as Katherine herself. Well, *she* would do everything in her power to make his stay pleasant and to follow out Katherine's desires.

So she hurried to the kitchen to see that everything was just as she knew Katherine wanted it. She saw that the crushed fruit was chilled, that the salad was crisp, that the fried chicken was piping hot. The long table looked lovely, she admitted. Just before she called them in, Mother pulled the shades down part way, so that the room seemed "peaceful — you know, like twilight."

They all came trooping in, Father continuing what he had evidently begun on the porch, a cheerful monologue on the income tax law. Bob and Mabel, who had arrived with the new baby in the reed cab that Father had given them, held a prolonged discussion as to where the cab and its wonderful contents could most safely stand during dinner.

With that old-fashioned notion that "menfolks like to talk together," Mother placed Keith Baldridge and Bob and Grandpa up at the end of the table by Father.

As they were being seated, Father said in that sprightly way which always came to him when a royal repast confronted him, "What's the matter with the curtains?" Then walking over to the windows with the highly original remark, "Let's have more light on the subject," he snapped the shades up to the limit. The June sun laughed fiendishly at Mother as it flashed across the cut glass and china and the huge low bowl of golden nasturtiums. Mother felt like shaking Father, but of course she couldn't get up and jerk the shades down again, like Xanthippe or Mrs. Caudle.

Tillie, with an exaggerated tiptoeing around the table, began passing the plates as Father served them. Previously, there had been a little tilt between Mother and Katherine over the coffee, the latter wanting it served at the close of the meal, "like real people," but Mother had won with, "Father would just ask for it, Kathie, so what's the use?" And now Tillie was saying hospitably, "Will you have coffee, Mr. Bald— Bald—?" At which Junior snorted in his glass of water, and received the look of a lieutenant-colonel from Mother.

There was a little interval of silence as the dinner started, then Grandpa looked down the table toward Katherine and said in his old, cracked voice, "Well, Tattern!" It was her childish nickname, put away on the shelf with her dolls and dishes. It sounded particularly silly to-day. "What you goin' to do with yourself now you've graduated?"

"I'm going to teach in the Miles City High School, Grandfather." She had never said Grandfather before; he'd always been "Grandpa" to her, but the exigencies of the occasion seemed to call for the more dignified term.

"What you goin' to teach?"

"History," she said briefly, and flushed to the roots of her hair. Marcia and Eleanor exchanged knowing grins.

"Then git married, I s'pose, and hev no more use fer your history? That makes me think of somethin' that happened back in Illynois. It was a pretty big thing fer anybody from our neck of the woods to go to college, but Abner Hoskins went, and when he was 'most through he got drowned. At the funeral Old Lady Stearns walked round the casket and looked down at the corpse 'n' shook her head 'n' said: 'My! My! What a lot o' good larnin' gone to waste.' "

Every one laughed. Katherine's own contribution to the general fund was of a sickly, artificial variety.

"You came here from Illinois at an early date, I suppose, Mr. Warner?" Keith Baldridge asked.

It was like a match to dynamite — no, like a match to a straw stack, a damp straw stack that would burn all afternoon. Grandpa looked as pleased as a little boy.

"*Yes,* sir — it was 1865. I fought with the old Illynois boys first, 'n' then I loaded up and come, with teams of course. That was a great trip, that was. Yes, *sir!* I mind, fer instance, how we crossed a crick with a steep bank, and the wagon tipped over, 'n' our flour — there was eight sacks — spilled in the water. Well, sir, would you believe them sacks of flour wasn't harmed, we got 'em out so quick? The water 'n' flour made a thin paste on the outside 'n' the rest wasn't hurt. I rec'lect the youngsters runnin' barelegged down the crick after Ma's good goosefeather pillows that was floating away."

Two scarlet spots burned on Katherine's cheeks. She raised miserable eyes that had been fixed steadily upon her plate to see Keith Baldridge looking at Grandpa in amazement. What was he thinking? Comparing Grandpa with his own father, dignified and scholarly?

On and on went Grandpa. "Yes, sir — the year I'm tellin' you about now was the year the grasshoppers come, 1874."

Marcia kicked Katherine under the table. "Same old flock has arrived," she whispered.

"They come in the fall, you know, 'n' et the corn, 'n' then the gol-durn things had the gall to stay all winter 'n' hatch in the spring. Why, there wasn't nothin' raised that summer but broom-corn 'n' sorghum-cane. You'd be surprised to know they left them two things." There was a great deal more information about the grasshoppers, and then: "Yes, sir, me'n Ma had the first sod house in Cass County. 'N' poor! Why, Job's turkey belonged in Rockefeller's flock by the side o' us. I had one coat, 'n' Ma one dress, fer I don't know how long, 'n' Molly over there" — he pointed with his knife to Mother, who smiled placidly back — "Molly had a little dress made outen flour sacks. The brand of flour had been called 'Hellas,' like some foreign country — Eyetalian or somethin'. Ma got the words all outen the dress but the first four letters of the brand, 'n' there it was right across Molly's back 'H-E-L-L,' 'n' Ma had to make some kind o' knittin' trimmin' to cover it up."

Every one laughed hilariously, Mother most of all. Junior shouted as though he were in a grandstand. Katherine gave a very good imitation of a lady laughing while taking a tablespoonful of castor oil.

"Well, Grandpa!" It was Father, when he could speak again. "She's had several dresses of later years that cost like that, but I never saw the word actually printed out on them."

Oh, it was awful! What would he think? He was laughing — but of course he would laugh! He was the personification of courtesy and tact. Talk about Wagner — "Il Penseroso" — Rodin! To Katherine's sensitive mind there stood behind Keith Baldridge's chair a ghostly, sarcastically-smiling group of college professors, ministers, lawyers, men in purple knickers and white wigs and plumed hats — gentlemen — aristocrats — patricians.

Behind her own chair stood sweaty farmers with scythes, white-floured millers, woodsmen with axes over their shoulders, rough old sea-captains — common folks — *plebeians.*

Her heart was an icicle within her. All the old longing for Keith Baldridge, all the desire to be near him, died out. With a sickening feeling that she was living in a nightmare, she only wanted the day to be over, so that he would go home, so that she could go to the cool dimness of her own room and be alone.

The dinner was over. Father, with the same nonchalance that he would have displayed had he been dining the Cabinet members, walked coolly into the library, and with the automobile section of the paper over his face prepared to take his Sunday nap.

Katherine, unceremoniously leaving Mr. Baldridge to the rest of the family, slipped out to the kitchen to wipe dishes for Mother and Tillie.

"Why, Kathie, you go right back!" Mother insisted.

"Let me be," she said irritably. "I know what I want to do."

Mother, giving her eldest daughter a swift look, had a savage desire to take her across her knee and spank her, even as in days of yore.

The work done, Katherine walked slowly up the back stairs, bathed and powdered her flushed face, and with a feeling that life held nothing worth while went down to join the family. As she stopped in the vestibule and surveyed the scene it seemed to her that it could not have been worse.

The porch seemed as crowded with people as a street fair. Father had finished his nap, and was yawning behind his paper. Eleanor's entire crowd of high school girls had stopped for her to take the Sunday afternoon walk which took place whether the thermometer stood at zero or 102° in the shade. They were all sitting along on top of the stone railing like a row of magpies.

Bob was wheeling the baby up and down, Mabel watching him, hawk-eyed, as though she suspected him of harboring intentions of tipping the cab over. Mother, red faced from the dinner work, was calling cheerily to a neighbor woman, "You've lots of grit to get out in this hot sun." Marcia, in the living-room, had just finished "The Mill on the Cliff" record, and was starting "The Sextette from Lucia," the fanfare of the trumpets literally tearing the air.

Grandpa, for Keith Baldridge's benefit, was dilating on the never-ending subject of grasshoppers. As he paused, Tillie, in her best black silk, came around the corner of the porch and sat down near the guest with "Be you any relation to the Baldridges down in East Suffolk, Connecticut?" (Oh, *what* would he think of Tillie, who had waited on him, doing that?) Junior, on the other side of Mr. Baldridge, was making frantic attempts to show him a disgusting eel in an old fish globe that was half full of slimy green water. Even the Maltese cat was croqueting herself in and out through Professor Baldridge's legs. To Katherine's hypersensitive state of mind the confusion was as though all Chinatown had broken out.

With a feeling of numb indifference, she stepped out on the porch. Keith Baldridge rose nimbly to his feet. "Now, good people," he said pleasantly, apparently unabashed, "I'm going to take Miss Katherine away for a while in the car. You'll all be here, will you, when I get back?"

Katherine went down the steps with him, no joy in her heart — nothing but a sense of playing her part callously in a scene that would soon end.

It was outrageously hot in the car. "How about going where it's cooler. Is there some woodsy place around here?" he wanted to know.

So Katherine obediently directed him to Springtown's prettiest picnic spot and, almost without conversation, they made a run for its beatific shade. As they walked over to the bank of the river, the man said, "I'm certainly elated over the find I made to-day."

"Find?" Katherine questioned politely.

"Yes — your grandfather. He's a wonderful man. He's promised to come to my home next week and stay several days with me. He's just what I've been looking for, an intelligent man who has lived through the early history of the state and whose memory is so keen that he can recall hundreds of anecdotes. I am working on a history of the state, and my plan is to have it contain stories of vividness and color, little dramatic events which are so often omitted from the state's dull archives. From the moment he began to talk I realized what a gold mine I had struck. I could scarcely refrain from having a pad and pencil in my hand all the time I was listening to him. Why, he's a *great* character — one of the typical pathfinders — sturdy, honorable, and lovable. You must be very proud of him."

"I — am," said Katherine feebly.

"Take, for instance, my chapter on the early political life of the state. Do you know he told me that one election day, when it came time for the polls to close, every one in the locality had voted but himself. He was miles away, hauling merchandise home from the river. A man got on a horse, rode over into the next county to meet him, then they exchanged places, your grandfather hurrying home on horseback while they held open the polls for him. It so happened that when the votes were counted, there had been a tie and, of course, his vote had decided the issue. Now, isn't that rich?"

Miss Mason acknowledged that it was.

"I'm a little cracked on the subject of these old pioneers," he went on. "To me they were the bravest, the most wonderful people in the world. Look at it!" He threw out his arm to the scene beyond the river. Before them, like a checkerboard, stretched the rolling farmland of the great Mid-West: brown squares of newly plowed ground; vivid green squares of corn; dull green squares where alfalfa was growing! Snuggled in the cozy nests of orchards were fine homes and huge barns. The spires of three country churches pointed their guiding fingers to the blue sky.

"Think of it! To have changed an immense area of Indian-inhabited wild land into this! Visualize to yourself, in place of what you see, a far-reaching stretch of prairie land on every side of us, with only the wild grass rippling over it. Now imagine this: you and I are standing here alone in the midst of it, with nothing but a prairie schooner containing a few meager necessities by our side. We're here to stay. From this same prairie we must build our home with our own hands, wrest our food, adequately clothe ourselves. It is to be a battle.

We must conquer or be conquered. Would you have courage to do it?" He turned to her with his fine, frank smile. And into Katherine Mason's heart came the swift, bitter-sweet knowledge that she could make sod houses and delve in the earth for food and kill wild animals for clothing — with Keith Baldridge.

"And this," he went on again, indicating the landscape, "this is our heritage from the pioneers. From sod houses to such beautiful homes as yours! I can't tell you how much I've enjoyed being in your family to-day. It's the typical happy American family. When I think of my own gloomy boyhood, I could fight some one — a lonesome, motherless little tad studying manners and 'Thanatopsis' under a tutor. Yours is the kind of home I've always wanted. It's the kind of home I mean to have when — if — I marry — all sunshine — and laughter — and little children —"

He turned to her suddenly and caught her hands. "It was to talk about that home that I brought you out here. With my whole heart — I love you — Katherine —"

It was late afternoon when the long gray car turned into the Mason driveway and stopped at the side lawn. In fact, it was so much later than Keith Baldridge had planned to leave that he only took time to run up to the porch to say good-by to them all. If he expected the Masons to sit calmly on the porch when he should drive away, he did not yet know the Masons. One and all, excepting Grandpa, who stayed in his rocker, they followed him down the steps, flocking across the green sloping lawn to where his car stood. The cat, seeing the entire family trooping in one direction, came bounding across the yard, tail in air, and rubbed herself coquettishly against the departing guest's trousers. She may have been of a curious disposition, that cat; but she was the soul of hospitality.

Tillie came running from the back of the house with a shoebox tied with a string. "It's some chicken sandwiches and cake," she explained. "Come again. I'll fry chicken for you any day."

Keith Baldridge beamed at her, and shook her rough hand vigorously. "I'm mighty glad to hear you say that, for you're going to have a chance to do that very thing next Sunday."

They all shook hands with him a second time. He got into the car and pressed the button that gave life to the monster. The wheels seemed quivering to turn. Just then Grandpa rose from his chair on the porch and excitedly waved his cane. "Say!" he called. He came hobbling over the grass, the late summer sun touching his scraggly gray hair. "Wait a minute, Mr. Baldridge!"

They all turned to watch him apprehensively, he seemed so hurried and anxious. He was close to the family group now. "Say! Mr. Baldridge! I jes' happened to think of somethin' else about them darned grasshoppers!"

They all shouted with laughter — all but Katherine, for she was not there. She had slipped into the front door and up to her room. There she dropped on her knees by the side of her bed and made a fervent little prayer to the God of Families. And her prayer was this: that some day — if she lived humbly for the rest of her life — she might be purged from the sin of having been, even in thought, disloyal to Her Own.

Then, hearing the family back on the porch, she rose from her knees and went into the hall. There she leaned over the banisters and called: "Mother! Come up here. I want you."

CHAPTER IV

TILLIE CUTS LOOSE

After Keith Baldridge's visit, the days slipped into that type of hot summer known to the Mid-West as "cracking good corn weather." As one after another of the torrid days passed Tillie began giving evidence of that same in-growing restlessness that had characterized those other periods prior to her decision to leave the Masons and make her home with relatives.

"One of these days I'm goin' to cut loose," she would hint with deep mystery.

Mother smiled, but seldom encouraged her. On one of those other occasions, years before, Mother had agreed with Tillie and encouraged her to try a change for awhile. At which Tillie had suddenly broken out into a wild and distressed sniveling. "I can see right through you," she had cried into her gingham apron. "You're sick of me livin' here."

"You certainly have to handle Tillie with gloves," Mother had said wearily to Father then, and she had said it many times since.

"By cricky! They'd be boxing-gloves if I had it to do," Father would return. Men are like that. If only they had the management of the hired help, you understand, all they would need to do would be to go into the kitchen and rant around and settle things once for all. It follows that things certainly would be settled.

This summer, Tillie seemed to Mother's keen eyes to be changing. From an almost fierce loyalty — in spite of frequent arguments — Tillie seemed to have acquired a frank disdain for many of Mother's ideas. She began going away several evenings in the week with no comment as to her destination, hitherto an unheard-of thing. Mother said nothing, but felt that something unusual must be possessing Tillie's mind. She obtained an inkling of what it was when Bob and Mabel, coming in for the evening, asked what Tillie was doing so much over at the Perkinses'.

She was sure of the reason later on a rainy afternoon, when she went into Tillie's room to close the windows. On Tillie's dresser lay an accumulation of reading material of the latest cult in which Mrs. Perkins had become interested.

Mrs. Perkins had lived in Springtown all her married life, but she had never taken root.

She had always been poised for flight, as it were, although a quarter of a century had gone by and two of the four children (who had miraculously brought themselves up) were married. She still maintained an air of fluttering condescension toward the town. Periodically she told her fellow citizens that the family would be moving to Capitol City soon now, and she confided to strangers that she was not really of Springtown, that she was but temporarily quartered there, and that her real life was lived in the outside world, to which she flew when the narrow limits of the town seemed choking her. As an opiate to soothe her in the winter of her discontent, she delved into the study of various creeds. Add as one cannot thoroughly detect the origin of cults and cobwebs at the same time, Mrs. Perkins's house contained as many of the one as the other.

With characteristic forbearance Mother maintained the friendliest of attitudes toward her, but admitted to a teasing family that she was "a little odd."

"Odd! Your grandmother!" the girls would say. "She's got bats in her belfry."

And now Tillie was apparently absorbed in the study of one of this peculiar woman's peculiar cults. Mother sighed as she went downstairs. It was difficult for her to understand how any one could need an addition to or an amplification of her own simple creed: "Whatsoever thy hand findeth to do —"

Tillie spoke about it herself in a few days. She and Mother were canning blackberries in a steaming hot kitchen that was full of the sickish-sweet odor of the fruit.

With characteristic shortness Tillie blurted out, "Molly, I might's well tell you first as last — I've decided to go away for good."

Mother, of course, was partially prepared for the news, but she did not say so. She only asked calmly, "What are your plans, Tillie?"

"Well — I ain't sure yet, but I'm goin' to do something for myself. I got some money, and there's things a-plenty that women can do these days. It's the age of woman. She's come into her own."

Mother could scarcely suppress a smile. Tillie's voice had that formal, stilted sound of quoting.

"I've lived here for eighteen years, Molly," she went on, "and in the next eighteen I'm goin' to do somethin' more broadenin'. You know yourself the town's little, and everybody here is livin' little cramped lives. I'm goin' to get out where things are bigger and" — she paused and then took the unfamiliar, icy plunge — "where I can stretch my soul."

The saying was so distinctly Perkinesque

that Mother had to turn abruptly to the sink to hide the unholy mirth on her face.

"Take yourself, for instance, Molly," the rasping, monotonous voice went on. "Mis' Perkins — she's certainly the broadest-minded woman I ever knew — she was talkin' about you to me, and she says just to look at Mis' Mason; you was bright and smart, and yet you'd just let yourself be tied down to the family all these years and never hardly traveled, like she had, to broaden out — and that you'd made a big mistake to let the children take all your time — and she says the very fact that you *like* Springtown showed that it had kept you too narrow to know different."

Two bright pink spots, neither of heat nor blackberry juice, burned on Mother's cheeks.

"Well, my studyin' these things with her — and I honestly wish you'd study them, too, Molly, you ain't rightly understood what this bein' cramped down means to you — it's made me decide to break away and get out. As I said, I got some money and I ain't called on to be nobody's under dog."

Mother silently clamped on a refractory jar cover. Not until she felt herself well enough in hand to speak calmly, did she ask quietly, "Where will you go, Tillie?"

"I'm plannin' first to go to Capitol City to

get me some new clothes — Mis' Perkins has good ideas on that, too — then I'm goin' up to Big Moon Lake with her. We're goin' to live at the Inn a week or two and meet some ladies there that Mis' Perkins has been correspondin' with. She's never met them, but they've all been studyin' this new thought, it's called cosmic philosophy, and course that makes us all friends to start with. After that, I'll decide just what I am goin' to do; I may go on to Chicago. But one thing's certain, Molly, Mis' Perkins has been the means of me seein' Springtown like it really is — and the narrow way we all live here."

Mother's part of the work was over. She slipped silently out of the kitchen, climbed the wide, curving stairway, and went into her room. Then she turned the lock and sat down in a low rocking-chair by the window. She was resentfully, flamingly angry, as good, high-minded people sometimes become angry. She was deeply, quiveringly hurt, as sensible, sunshiny people, who do not go about looking for slights, are sometimes hurt.

If Mrs. Perkins had said it directly to her, she would have made light of it and put it aside. If Tillie, by some miraculous mental exertion, had thought it up herself, Mother could even have laughed at it. But to undermine Tillie's regard for her in that subtle way, turn

72

her old friend and helper from her, after all these years of working side by side!

"Keep calm, now," Mother said mentally. "Look at this thing fairly. Mrs. Perkins has traveled about a great deal. Maybe there is some truth in what she says." That same calm hold upon her other self, who was both impulsive and tempery, had seen Mother safely through many a trial.

Was she narrow?

It is a very big question, that deciding who is narrow and who broad-minded. Broad-mindedness knows no financial standing nor rank of station. Bigotry is limited neither to rural communities nor cities. There are narrow-minded poor people and broad-minded millionairies, just as there are liberal-minded country storekeepers and smug, provincial-minded Congressmen.

In retrospect, Mother began looking back over the years of her married life. How she had endeavored to keep her mind fresh and open! Even in the days when they had lived across town in the first tiny cottage that seemed full of tumbling babies, she had never allowed a day to pass without a few hurriedly snatched moments of good reading. Though clothes were mended and turned and made over, yet there were always good books and magazines on the table.

Sudden, hot tears rushed to her eyes at the recollection of the children piling into bed, and the thought of herself, tired to the depths with the work and confusion, wandering with them through all the dear old childhood tales.

With that alacrity with which the mind leaps from one memory to another, she thought of the set of travel books for which she had paid the sum of forty-five dollars in the days when that sum was a huge one. Whimsically she remembered the shabby old gray coat and velvet toque she had worn a winter longer than they seemed even passably decent, because of the books. She wondered if in Mrs. Perkins's long trips, born of discontent and unwillingness to keep a home sweet and lovely, there had been half the satisfaction that she herself had obtained from those precious volumes.

Travel? No, Mother had not traveled. A few short trips limited to the mid-west states themselves, and the one long journey she and Father had taken to the western coast completed the meager list. Washington! New York! Boston! It was with a distinct shock that she realized she had never seen them. It seemed almost unbelievable, for New York's famous sky line, the interesting old places in Boston, her country's capital, all seemed as pleasantly familiar to her as the streets of Springtown.

Mother had that peculiar God-given gift of imagination so keen that the printed word became to her a vivid, living reality. It was as though, while her body stayed at home and cared for the children, her spirit had climbed far mountain peaks and sailed into strange harbors.

Because of Barrie and Kipling and scores of others she had been intimately, sensitively in touch with the places and peoples of the world. She had stood on wind-swept, heather-grown Scottish moors, and broken bread in the little gray homes of the Thrums weavers. She had watched, fascinated, the slow-moving, red-lacquered bullock carts, veiled and curtained, creep over the yellow-brown sands of India. She had walked under brilliant stars down long, long trails in clear, cold, silent places, and she had strolled through groves of feathery flowering loong-yen trees of China. She had sensed to the fin-ger tips the beauty of the witching, seductive moon-filled nights of Hawaii, and with strained eyes and chilling heart she had watched for the return of the fishing fleet on the wild-wind banks of Labrador.

Yes, the warp of Mother's life had been restricted to keeping the home for Henry and the children. But the woof of the texture had been fashioned from the wind clouds and star drifts of the heavens.

As she had touched her life with all the lives of these peoples of the earth, for the time being sunk her own personality in theirs, she had come to the conviction that, fundamentally, there was nothing in life that could not be found in this little inland town.

Narrow? She looked out of her windows over the pleasant maple-edged, elm-bordered streets, where the warm afternoon sun cast little quivering glints of gold. In that bungalow over there she had assisted when a child was born. In the big house across the street she had helped manage the wedding supper for a glowing bride. Down in that old-fashioned wing-and-ell she had closed the eyes of an old man in his last long sleep. Narrow? Was birth narrow? Or marriage? Or death?

For a long time she sat rocking, thinking of the twenty-six years spent in the tiny town which, after all, was a cross-section of life. And if she made a little prayer: "O, Lord, keep me clean of heart — clear of mind — sweet of soul — gentle of speech" it was because she had tested the Source of her strength many times before.

She rose, bathed, dressed in fresh linens, as though to leave in the laundry basket all the disturbing thoughts of the past hour. She combed her graying hair carefully, put on a beautifully laundered blue house dress and little ruffled apron, and then, calm, placid, serene, came out of her room. And there was about her a little of the spirit of the Man who, long ago, came out of a Garden.

In the evening, Tillie, with the literature that was guaranteed to give such breadth of mind, left the house for Mrs. Perkins's.

The entire Mason family was congregated in the library, Bob and Mabel having come in with the baby. There was the usual diversity of occupations with the usual resultant confusion. Mother, who was deftly inclosing a large space of air in the knee of Junior's stocking, looked up to say quite casually:

"Folks, Tillie is going to leave us."

"Leave! What for? Why?" The chorus was in perfect unison, as though the family had been drilled.

"She wants," said Mother soberly, but with her eyes twinkling, "to stretch her soul."

Every one surveyed her in blank astonishment.

"Stretch her soul!" Eleanor repeated, "what in the *world* is that?"

"I don't know," Mother said demurely; "but she wants to do it."

"Oh, I know," Katherine volunteered, "it's some of that slush Mrs. Fat Perkins has been telling her. We might be in the wrong sphere, you know, and be mentally confined and never know it. It's only by getting out into — er — cosmic spaces or something like that — that we find out whether we've really been contented or not."

"Imagine Tillie rattling around in a cosmic space," Marcia contributed.

"What's a cosmetic space?" Junior wanted to know, which was the signal for a lusty shout from every one.

"She told me," Mother explained, "that she's cramped here in Springtown, and she wants to get out and do something for herself."

Father looked over the top of his paper. Father was one of those men who have apartment-house brains, the party that lives on the lower floor being able to read and digest all the international news while the one on the upper floor constantly sticks his head out of the window and hears all the household gossip.

"Well," he said cheerfully, "as one of our presidents said, 'Every nation is entitled to self-determination.' And if nations, why not Tillie?"

"Sure!" Bob put in. "Tillie is just up to date, looking for her place in the sun."

Marcia chuckled. "Believe *me,* she'd make a bigger hit if it was in the *dark* 'o the *moon.*"

The young folks all laughed.

"Children! Children!" Mother admonished them. Then she sighed. Never could she stay the inrolling tide of comments when the Masons with unity attacked a subject.

One week later Tillie left. Her last words were the suggestion that Mother hire the Dority girl to help her, and added, by way of reference, "Though land knows, she don't know beans when the bag's open."

Mother missed Tillie as the late summer days passed. The girls made elaborate promises to take her place so that Mother would not feel the lack of help. But any one who has raised three pretty, popular daughters will know that the sum of the combined tasks done by them was not equal to the faithful service of Tillie, who was neither pretty nor popular.

At the end of the second week the Masons were at the supper table when they heard some one coming up the front steps, and through the wide front hall. In the dining room doorway stood Tillie, the Prodigal. She had on a new navy blue suit of the latest cut. A chic little hat with scarlet cockade, that would have becomingly adorned the head of a movie star, was slipping about rakishly on Tillie's flat hair.

"Here I be," she said bluntly, sourly.

There was a chorus of welcoming voices that

brought a dull red to the wanderer's high-boned cheeks. Mother rose from her chair, and with outstretched hands went swiftly toward her.

"Good land, Molly!" — Tillie seemed genuinely distressed — "I hope you ain't goin' to kiss me."

Mother laughed girlishly. "No, I wouldn't dare, Tillie; but you can rest assured I *feel* like it."

"Did you hire that silly little Dority girl?" was Tillie's next question.

"No," said Mother, "we didn't even try to get her. The girls have helped me." Somewhere the god of Tact gave Mother credit for the reservation of the words "a little." "I *hope* you're going to stay?"

"I be," she answered curtly.

They could get no more out of her until she was through supper. Then she pushed back her chair and said, "Now, I'm agoin' to tell you somethin'. I could keep it to myself I s'pose, and I'll prob'ly wish I had — but I ain't goin' to, for I want to get it off my chest. Only I don't want one o' you to ever throw it up to me again as long as I live. I went to Capitol City, and I got me some new clothes, and I ain't begrudgin' the money, for I felt tonier than I ever did in my life before. I had my face manicured, too."

Several of the Masons simultaneously dropped their napkins and dived under the table for them.

"That was a powerful fussy job, and it's the first and last time I'll ever let anybody hit me in the face with a fly-slapper. I wouldn't a-cared if I'd looked any different when they got through with me; but it's the Lord's truth, girls, I didn't look one mite changed, and that face-manicurin' business is all a hold-up."

"Well, of course, Tillie, it *is* a *skin* game," Marcia put in, which gave every one a chance to let off some laughter. Tillie did not crack a smile.

"Then I met Mis' Perkins at Big Moon Lake, and I don't mind sayin' I felt about as good as any one with my new clothes. The first morning after we got there we was sittin' on a seat by a big tree, and some eight or nine ladies and girls came along and stopped near us. They were nice-dressed, nice-lookin' women, and we guessed right away that they was the ladies from the philosophy school, and so we talked to the one nearest us. She said she was expectin' us. The others had started on ahead by that time, and she told us to come along as they was out sight-seein', goin' to look at the rapids and climb one of the hills. So we walked along with her and all this time she and Mis' Perkins talked, but lots deeper and queerer than anything I'd read yet, and I got kinda sick of so much of it at a stretch. But Mis' Perkins seemed to be just in her element.

"We walked around lookin' at the places of interest and about noon got back to the Inn lawn. Then one of the ladies who had been pointin' out all the places to us come to Mis' Perkins and me and pulled us aside and said she hadn't noticed us joinin' the crowd in the rear in the mornin' until we got part way up the hill. Then she said she hadn't wanted to embarrass us when she did see us, so she waited till we got back to tell us that these ladies was all from the sanitarium near by, and though they was harmless they wasn't any of 'em right in their minds. I can't see nothin', very funny about it myself, but I know all of you well enough to know it's the kind of thing you laugh your heads off over. So, laugh!" she said shortly, crabbedly.

Tillie's supposition was entirely correct. The Mason family laughed until it wept.

When they were in shape to hear her again, she finished with: "I made up my mind right then and there, if I couldn't tell crazy folks from the students of the philosophy I was studyin', I'd come back to Springtown, where we know Grandma McCabe and Silly Johnson are the only loony ones in town, unless," she added acridly, "you count Mis' Perkins, too."

The next morning, Tillie in her stiffly starched gingham dress stopped by the kitchen clock shelf.

"What's these?" She picked up some oblong slips of paper and glared at Mother.

"Oh," Mother responded timidly, "those are your checks." Then she added naïvely, "They've sort of accumulated up there, haven't they?"

"What have I got checks for?"

"Why, I put one up there every Saturday you were gone."

"You thought I'd come back?"

"I *knew* it." Mother was growing braver. "Don't you suppose I know that you need me just as much as I need you? I'm in hopes you'll make your home here with us the rest of your life, and when the children are all gone, and you and I are two decrepit old ladies, you can wait on me part of the time and I can wait on you the other part. In the meantime, I can pay your regular salary to your body — can't I? — while your soul takes a little vacation."

For the second time in the eighteen years Tillie surprisingly threw her gingham apron over her head and burst into a loud and distressed sniveling. "Molly Mason," she wailed, "you're the very best woman that ever walked on the top of the Lord's green earth."

Tender-hearted Mother, who had been hunting for a handkerchief and couldn't locate one, wiped her eyes on a tennis-flannel kettle holder. "Oh, no, Tillie," she said tremulously, "not that — just ordinarily decent."

Suddenly Tillie pulled the apron off her head, raised her distorted face and broke forth into a high, weird, henlike cackle. "Oh, my land-a-Goshen!" she chortled, "stretchin' my soul! *Ain't I a fool?*"

"I'm certainly glad Tillie's back," Mother said complacently to Father that night in their room.

Father finished a yawn. Then he dropped a large heavy shoe that made a large heavy thud. He, too, was glad Tillie was back, for Mother's sake. As for himself, he had fared quite comfortably while Tillie was gone.

"Well, how about her soul?" he asked. "Has it been stretched?"

"Yes," Mother answered, smilingly emphatic, "it has. It has been stretched enough to let in a faint glimmering of genuine humor."

"By golly! She needed some," Father returned. Then he yawned and dropped the other shoe.

CHAPTER V

THE THEATRICAL SENSATION

Just a few weeks later, when the goldenrod was spreading its yellow lace to trim the edges of the cornfield, and the blue of the gentians was vying for brilliancy with the scarlet of the sumac, Katherine left for her first year of teaching in Miles City, Marcia for her senior year at college, and Eleanor and Junior returned to their studies in the home school.

Father and Mother held the sensible view that each of the girls should take up some practical training, so Marcia had chosen a course in primary teaching.

"How'd you happen to choose primary?" Katherine had asked her.

"Oh, primary hours are shortest of all, and who wants to stay in a schoolroom any longer than he has to?" had been Marcia's cheerful reply. And when you come to think about it — who does?

Not until the Thanksgiving vacation did the entire family get together again. There were a great many experiences related in those few days. Katherine's report was one of intense seriousness over the young history students who sat in her classes. Marcia's account of her work was not of such a solemnity.

"In October we taught those little Comanches about squirrels and Columbus and other adventurous gentlemen," she announced blithely to the family, and added with bland unconcern: "Primary teachers are awful liars. Imagine this!' The whole month has been rainy, and we've had to smile our mail-order smiles and make those youngsters sing 'Pit-a-pat, see the *lovely* raindrops,' just because it was supposed to have mutual relation to the disgusting elements."

Eleanor, in the meantime, had been deep in one of those sticky, quagmire attachments for a teacher into which a high school girl often slips. It was a barnaclelike adherence that continued after Thanksgiving. The teacher's name was Buckwalter — Miss Genevieve Buckwalter, and her mind contained a great many convolutions that had been made by romantic experiences. Her life, so far, had been divided, like all Gaul, into three parts, which centered respectively about the following characters:

1. The man she had wanted to marry.
2. The man who had wanted to marry her.

3. The man she was going to marry.

Miss Buckwalter taught the English Literature class. And because she was capable of making an extra credit, Eleanor Mason, sixteen and a junior, was scheduled to take English Literature with the seniors. From this class Miss Buckwalter organized the Shakespeare Club, and so cleverly did she manipulate matters that when the members signed the constitution — which document was nearly as long and serious looking at the Constitution of the U. S. — it was discovered that there were just fourteen members, evenly divided as to sex.

"That will give them more interest in the club," said Miss Buckwalter. Which deduction showed amazing wisdom.

The Shakespeare Club met every other Friday night in Miss Buckwalter's pretty suite of rooms. And, to make the club more attractive to the young people, she served refreshments. On the way home after the first meeting, tall, lanky Frank Marston said, gosh, he wished she'd speed up a little on the eats, that the part of his wafer that didn't stick in his teeth flew down the front of his coat. But, take it all in all, the club flourished like the cedars of Lebanon.

Thereafter, Eleanor Mason's language was not the language of her forbears. From morning until night she dropped sayings of the immortal bard. She answered every innocent question with a flippant Stratford-on-Avon answer. The family accepted it as they had the measles, an epidemic that, heaven willing, would be over some day.

After school hours, immediately following the banging of the front door, they would hear, " 'Oh, Jupiter, how weary are my spirits!' "

To Father's grumbling about Old Man Smith not tending the furnace to suit him, Eleanor said:

"Fret till your proud heart break.
Go, show your slaves how choleric you are,
And make your bondsmen tremble."

A piece of gossip from Junior brought forth " *'Peace! Fool! Where learned you that'?"*

When Tillie came in to say that she believed on her soul when she lifted that wash water she had strained her back, Eleanor told her jauntily that the quality of mercy was not strained, that it droppeth as the gentle rain from heaven upon the earth beneath.

Tillie was disgruntled. "Can't that girl talk sense lately?" she wanted to know.

"Never mind her, Tillie," Father said. "She's only with us in the flesh — her spirit is living with the great international poet who cornered the market."

"Well, couldn't he a-wrote so white folks could have a chance to understand him?" Tillie retorted acridly.

Aside from these poetic flights, Eleanor was apparently unchanged. Mother watched her covertly to ascertain whether the boy question had presented itself. But, gay and carefree, after every club meeting Eleanor would bring in the half-dozen young people who lived nearest, and together they would eat large quantities of sandwiches in the Mason kitchen. But, "Better a lot of eating in the kitchen than a little sweethearting on the porch," was Mother's motto.

Then came great expectations. The club was to give a play in the spring. Miss Buckwalter evolved the idea that it would make a great hit, be good training for the students, and bring in a mint of money for the school library. Thereupon she chose "Romeo and Juliet." And because of Eleanor Mason's keen intelligence, and the fact that her father was president of the school board and would appreciate the honor, Miss Buckwalter selected her for Juliet. She might have spared herself any pains on account of the latter reason, for a duck's back was not more impervious to water than Father to the fact that he had been highly honored.

Mother was disgusted. "I'm provoked through and through," she told Father. For twenty-six years Father had been her exhaust pipe. " 'Romeo and Juliet!' How *perfectly* silly! I talked to Miss Jenkins — she's so sensible — she didn't approve either, said she suggested 'Merchant of Venice,' or 'As You Like It,' as lesser evils; but a road company gave the 'Merchant' here not long ago, and Miss Buckwalter said she couldn't fix a good forest of Arden when the trees were cut bare. She claims she will cut the play a great deal — but think of that balcony scene!" Mother threw up her hands despairingly. "Well, I'll not interfere; but you mark my word, Henry, Eleanor will get foolish notions in her head. Why, Father, she's only *sixteen*."

"Well, haven't I heard somewhere that the original Miss Capulet was fourteen?"

Seeing that Mother was too much perturbed to answer him, Father said cheerfully, "Oh, I wouldn't worry, Mother. Eleanor's the most sensible girl we've got, and the teacher will be there with them." Father was one of those old-fashioned souls who think, optimistically, that the teacher, like the king, can do no wrong. But Mother, having taught school herself, well knew that teachers were of the earth earthy.

Comes now Andrew Christensen. Andy had

arrived with his parents at Ellis Island from a small country noted for dairy products, some fifteen years before. And now, at nineteen, to prove that he was a genuine American, he dressed in the most faddish clothes and specialized in slang. In fact he was so much a man of the world that, so far as girls were concerned, he seldom deigned to waste his fragrance on the desert air of Springtown, preferring, at ball games, to flaunt various out-of-town girls before his classmates. Mornings before school and on Saturdays he worked in Thompson's combined grocery and meat market. He was big and blond and good-looking. And he was Romeo.

Rehearsals began. To Miss Buckwalter's disappointment, Eleanor Mason was not getting as much out of her part as she had anticipated. Words? Eleanor could reel them all off at the first rehearsal. But when she said, "Wherefore art thou Romeo? What's Montague? Is it nor hand nor foot? What's in a name?" she might as well, for all the heart she put in it, have said, "Do you like onions? Or prunes? Can you stand the sight of carrots?"

So, with much coaching on Miss Buckwalter's part and much faithful endeavor on Eleanor's, the practice went on. And then — quite suddenly — Eleanor needed no more coaching. They were on the drafty stage of the old opera house, Eleanor standing on a dry-goods box in lieu of a balcony. Andy reached up and took her hand for the first time. A little shiver, as delicious as it was strange, went through her.

" 'Wouldst thou withdraw thy vow?' " said Andy. " 'For what purpose, love?' "

And Eleanor, her honest little heart beating suffocatingly, leaned over the old box and answered softly:

"My bounty is as boundless as the sea,
My love as deep; the more I give to thee,
The more I have, for both are infinite."

And she meant it.

After that rehearsal Mother noted a subtle change in Eleanor. She seemed very subdued. She slipped up to her room a great deal to read. She became fussy about her clothes. She seemed (and Mother knew this to be the most genuine symptom) to have lost her sense of humor.

When Bob dropped in on his way home and wanted to know how Romeo and Julio were coming on, there was no merry crinkle around Eleanor's eyelids, only a very dignified answer from her.

Junior and the crowd of boys with whom

she had occasionally been wont to hobnob were as the dust beneath her feet. The Saturday before the play, they came into the house and entreated her long and noisily to come to the pasture and help them make up a nine. But their supplication was met with such withering scorn that when they left Junior stuck his head back in the door to deliver this cutting farewell: "All right for you, Lady Juliet De Snub Nose! You can put this in your pipe and smoke it — this is the last time us boys'll ever ask *you* to do a *darn thing!*"

As for Eleanor, she was living in the rarefied atmosphere which the new thing in her life had created. She walked daily in the land of Romance; but where she had hitherto only caught rare glimpses of a faraway shadowy creature, now he had come closer to her through the forest and, behold — it was Andy!

The night of the play, Springtown turned out as small towns always do for home talent and packed the old barnlike opera house to the doors.

The program opened with a piano solo by Marybelle Perkins. Probably Paderewski or Josef Hofmann could have done as well, but the Perkinses wouldn't have admitted it. Then the high school boys' Glee Club sang "Anchored," and when they ended with "Safe, safe at last, the harbor passed," people were so relieved that the boys were quite reasonably safe at last from their perilous musical journey that they applauded vigorously.

There was a short farce and then — The Play.

There was a great deal of loud and boisterous enmity displayed between the followers and retainers of the respective houses of Capulet and Montague. There was a scene, somewhat hilarious, showing the ball given by Lord Capulet. There was the balcony scene, and the grand finale of the poison and the dark tombs.

Springtown liked it. True, there were a few discrepancies. One might have been carried back to a long-gone generation on fleeter wings of imagination had he not, through the foliage on the side of the balcony, caught glimpses of "Mr. Tobias S. Thompson, Dealer in Meats and Fancy Groceries." One recognized the portly Mrs. John Marston's old purple velvet coat on her lanky son Frank, and Lord Montague displayed a startling combination of dress-suit coat and sixteenth-century legs. The tomb where lay the bones of the dead Capulets looked like a cross between an automobile hood and a dog kennel. But, taken as a whole, it was a very creditable performance.

Father and Mother Mason sat in the center

aisle, sixth row. Across from them sat Mr. and Mrs. Andrew Christensen, Sr., with so many little Christensens that it had taken nearly a day's wages to get tickets and reserved seats. Mr. Christensen was not yet far enough removed from kings and things but that he glowed with pride because Andy was playing opposite the banker's girl.

People whispered to each other that they never knew Eleanor Mason was so pretty. Lithe and lovely in her white costume, Juliet leaned over the balcony. In after years she was never to smell the pungent odor of rose geranium without seeing Andy's face, pale, a little tremulous, turned up to her.

Liquid-like, dulcet-toned, dripped Juliet's:

*Good night, good night. Parting is such
    sweet sorrow,
That I could say good night until the
    morrow.*

The audience clapped and clapped. Miss Buckwalter, in the wings, was elated. "Eleanor never did so well," she said to Miss Jenkins. Only Mother, sixth row, center, moaned over and over in her heart, "Oh, *what* have they done to my little girl?"

The play was over. The audience breathed a long sigh, rose, began laughing and talking.

Mother felt a fierce intuitive resentment against Andy. She did not want him to go home alone with her girl. So she used the only weapon of defense she knew, a sandwich. With a hasty mental calculation as to how many buns there would be left for the next day after dividing four dozen into fourteen boys and girls, she invited them all up to the house.

It was an incongruous sight — Romeo and Tybalt and the old nurse and Friar Lawrence, *en costume,* perched on the kitchen sink and table cabinet, devouring sandwiches. As they were leaving the kitchen, Mother made a casual survey of the trays, and discovered that the answer to her problem in mathematics was "Not any."

The Capulets and the Montagues all flocked out into the big hall. Andy hung back a moment to speak to Eleanor.

"Say, kid, I wanta see you in the morning when I bring the meat. I wanta ask you something when the mob ain't around."

There was only one thing it could mean, Eleanor told herself when she was alone in her room. It was a date for Sunday. She had never had a real "date," the boys just happened in at times. In an ecstasy of emotion she went to bed. For a long time she lay imagining what she would say to the girls when they came for her to go walking Sunday afternoon. She would answer carelessly, "I can't, girls. I'm sorry. Andy's coming."

When she woke with a start the sun was shining in her windows. All about her were evidences of the Great Event — her costume, a crumpled program, her roses in a jar in the hall. She dressed carefully in a softly frilled blue dress and sat down by the window to wait. She didn't want any breakfast. Eating? How commonplace!

There was a sound of the rattly cart that Andy drove. She wished Andy had a nicer job; he was intending to be a traveling man. She heard him go around the house and then, whistling cheerfully, coming back. She went to the window and raised it.

" 'But soft! What light through yonder window breaks?' " he called. " 'It is the east, and Juliet is the sun!' "

They both laughed. How easy it was to laugh with Andy.

"Come on down!" he called. "I want to ask you that."

On winged feet of hope, she sped down the front stairs. Andy perched on the stone railing of the big porch, his cap on the back of his blond, curly head.

"Well, Juliet, we're some little actors — what?"

At Eleanor's answering smile, he said: "Say,

97

kiddo, I wanta ask you to help me think of something for my girl's birthday. It's tomorrow and I'm going to see her. She lives over at Greenwood, and she's some swell dame, believe me. There's nobody in this town that's got a look-in with her. I thought maybe you could think of some nifty stunt."

Eleanor bent to her slipper for a moment, so that when she lifted her head it was quite natural that she looked flushed. Her heart was pounding terribly. She felt sick, but she forced a little crooked smile. There was sturdy pioneer blood in Eleanor, the strain that meets crises clear-eyed and bravely. So she said sturdily, "Why, Andy, flowers or books are nice."

"Nix on the flowers. You won't see little Andy loping up with a bunch of posies. And books — she likes sweller things than reading."

"You wouldn't want to get anything as expensive as a kodak, would you?"

"Sure thing, just the dope. You're some kid. I thought you'd know something right-o. Much obliged. Well, so long, kiddo. See you at the algebra funeral Monday morning."

The little wings of hope were bruised and bleeding when she dragged them back up the stairs. She closed her door and threw herself down on the floor by the window, a little crumpled heap. So this was the end! Andy hadn't meant any of those things he had said. He had sounded so honest and truthful. The beautiful new thing in her life was gone. The hot gushing tears of youth came. Sobs shook her.

Ah, well! At sixteen a broken dream is as cruel as a broken reality, for there is no one to tell you which is reality and which is dream.

As she sat battling with emotions that would not be laid low, she turned in desperation to the long shelf of books near by. Mechanically she reached for a fat little volume and turned the leaves. Here was one called "The Saddest Hour." With a vague hope that the eminently appropriate title would put her own painful thoughts into words, she began:

The saddest hour of anguish and of loss
Is not that moment of supreme despair
When we can find no least light anywhere —

Surely it couldn't be that life held sadder moments than this. She read hurriedly, avidly. What, then, was the saddest hour? It seemed it was not when we sup on salt of tears, nor even when we drink the gall of memories of days that have passed. Here it was:

But when with eyes that are no longer wet
We look out on the great wide world of men,

And, smiling, lean toward a bright
to-morrow —
To find that we are learning to forget —
Ah! then we face the saddest hour of
sorrow.

Then the saddest hour of all would never
come to her, for of course she would never,
never forget. For a long time she sat by the
window looking mournfully out on the bleak
landscape. There was some solace in the
thought of dying and being buried in her Juliet costume, with a sprig of rose geranium
in her hand. Andy would come and when he
saw her, dead, in her little white Juliet dress,
he'd think how rosemary was for remem-
brance. . . .

Junior and Runt Perkins and several of the
boys of that crowd were coming up the back
walk. They came close and stopped under the
clothesline. There were eight of them. They
were motioning to her. What did they want?
She put up her window.

"Oh, *El*-ner, come on down and make up
the nine. Shorty Marston had to go to Miles
City with his mother. Come on, please. *Please*
do, El-ner." Different voices were taking up
the refrain.

Eleanor leaned out. The air was mild and
damp as though somewhere there had been a

gentle rain. There was a faint smell of mellow loam everywhere. Down behind the garage the hens were cackling noisily. The trunks of the maple trees were moist with sap. There was a faint tinge of green on the hill beyond the pasture.

"You can pitch, El-ner, er bat," Runt Perkins called enticingly, "er any old thing."

"Well," she said suddenly, "wait till I change my dress and get a bite to eat."

At noon Father came up the walk proudly carrying the new broom that Mother had told him to get two weeks before. At the back porch he stopped and looked across the alley to the half block of pasture land where in summer he kept his cow. For a few moments he stood watching, then a grin came slowly over his face and he turned and went into the house.

"Mother," he said, "for once in your life you were good and mistaken about one of you offspring."

"Who's that?" Mother withdrew her rumpled head from a coat closet.

"Eleanor. All that Juliet stuff never fazed her. I told you she was the most sensible kid we had. She's out there in the pasture with Junior's bunch, and she's just made a home run. She took it like a sand-hill crane, her hair flying, and the boys cheering her like little Comanches."

"Well, thank the Lord," said Mother devoutly.

Out in the old pasture lot, the Jilted One was looking out on the great wide world of men, and smiling, and leaning toward a bright to-morrow.

CHAPTER VI

PROVING MARCIA TO HAVE BEEN BORN LUCKY

It was only a few weeks after the Shakespeare thriller that Katherine and Marcia came home for the spring vacation. To Mother the few days of their stay were very precious. Life was never the same with part of the family away.

Characteristically the two girls gave divergent reports of their work. After Katherine had given the family a comprehensive and earnest dissertation on the work she had accomplished, Marcia summed up her own strenuous mental labors with:

"We had a perfect orgy of cherry trees and hatchets and valentines in February — and I wish you could have seen the training school in March. We simply fell over seed boxes and kites, and we fairly *ate* pussywillows. This month we've painted millions of wild-looking robins. You'd die to see them — their beaks all run down and mix up sociably with their wings. It's a great life," she added blithely.

It was during this spring vacation that she began talking about Capitol City. "I'm just *living* to teach there next year. They send some member of the board every spring to the training school to choose the best teachers, and I *must* be one. I don't want to go to any little two-by-four burg. Capitol City for *me!* I ask an interest in your prayers."

So short was the brief week that the girls were gone again before Mother could realize the distressing fact. Part of Mother went with them. It is an acrobatic feat that only mothers can understand, this ability to be with every child.

To do Marcia justice, she really applied herself that spring when the stakes were worth working for. On the last Friday morning in April she had gone from the college to town on one of her numerous unimportant errands, and was waiting by the downtown station for the college car: As it stopped, a sorority sister came down the steps. "He's in there," she whispered. "Capitol City superintendent — come for teachers."

"Where?"

"There — halfway down — right-hand side."

He looked just as Marcia would have expected him to look — heavy, distinguished, gray-haired, with a Van Dyke beard. She sat down behind him and whispered to his broad back a foolish little jargon:

"Eeny meeny miny mo,
Please, kind sir, choose me to go."

Across the aisle from the great man sat Mrs. Hastings, the college doctor's wife. A strange young man was with her. From occasional glimpses of his good-looking profile, Marcia decided that he bore a faint resemblance to Mrs. Hastings. There was something about him she liked, his square jaw and alert manner and a distinct air of sophistication that none of the college boys had yet acquired.

The car stopped at the entrance to the campus and let out its load. As Marcia was about to pass Mrs. Hastings and the strange man, the former said, "Oh, Miss Mason, are you in a hurry?" As there was merely a small matter of an English Literature class due then, Miss Mason assured Mrs. Hastings she was not at all in haste.

"Could you show my brother around a little? My brother, Mr. Wheeler, Miss Mason. . . . I would go with him myself, but I told Hannah if the baby needed me, to put a red cloth in the window, and there it is!" She pointed excitedly to her home across from the campus. She was breathless, and anxious to get away.

"Maybe the baby has only joined the Bolsheviki," her brother suggested.

Marcia laughed. She liked him, his keen brown eyes and the sudden humorous lift to the mouth that she had thought so stern.

"You can see for yourself he's not married or he wouldn't be so flippant over a serious matter," Mrs. Hastings called to Marcia. "Show him the new amphitheater — and Science Hall" — she was already halfway across the street — "and the new dormitory and the training school."

"My sister," Mr. Wheeler said, "missed her calling. She would have made an excellent major general or park policeman."

Marcia laughed again. She still liked him. Mr. Wheeler looked down at his appointed guardian. She wore an immaculate white skirt with an audaciously green silk sweater and cap. The V-shaped neck of her blouse set off the lovely contour of her face. By way of completing a very satisfactory picture there was a bunch of dewy-sweet violets in her belt.

"Do you happen by any chance," Mr. Wheeler asked, "to be the Miss Mason who is Keith Baldridge's fiancée?"

"No, indeed," Miss Mason said, more emphatically than was necessary, for it wasn't at all disgraceful to be engaged to Keith Baldridge. "That's my sister Katherine. I'm Marcia. And you know Keith?"

"Like David knew Jonathan."

They crossed the green sloping campus, sweet-smelling from its recent mowing. There was some conversation relative to their mutual interest in Keith Baldridge, and then Marcia said glibly:

"You see before you the new Science Hall. It is thirty-seven stories high, a mile square and cost seventy million dollars. The roof of the new dormitory may be seen through the trees. Out beyond the Domestic Science building is the amphitheater and beyond the amphitheater — lies Italy."

They had come to a little rustic bridge across a miniature creek. Neither one made a move to walk on. In fact, to be explicit, they sat down on the low railing.

"As for the training school," Marcia continued, "I wouldn't voluntarily take you there. It's the place where you abandon hope all ye who enter here."

"You teach there?"

"I do." She looked at her wrist watch. "And in fifty minutes I'm to teach before the new superintendent of the Capitol City schools, if I haven't died of fright. He was on the car. Did you see him — a big husky Vandyker?" Mr. Wheeler had noticed him.

"I want to make a professional hit with him," Marcia went on confidentially. "I've simply got to teach in Capitol City next year. I *love* a city. I want to walk in the crowds and eat at tea-rooms. I want to go to the theater and sit in a box."

Mr. Wheeler looked judicially, appraisingly, at her. "I don't believe," he said soberly, "it would injure the looks of the box."

They both laughed. Marcia was enjoying herself immensely. He was like that for the whole hour they were together, keen, clever, interesting. In comparison with him all the home boys and college boys of her numerous friendships faded quietly into a blurred masculine background. In the light of his clever repartee Marcia reveled. To his questioning she told him a great deal about herself. She described faculty members to the last comic detail. Mr. Wheeler enjoyed it, apparently, so she made fun of the training school for his benefit. She spared no one. She mocked the artificial manners of the student teachers and imitated the head of the department. His hearty, virile laugh was ample payment for her pains.

It lacked seven minutes of the hour. Marcia slipped down from the bridge rail with "I go, like the quarry slave at night scourged to his dungeon." Suddenly she clapped her hand to her throat in a characteristic gesture. "Oh, my *goodness!* — I forgot — I have to get a whole violet plant with the roots on for my class. Oh, *help* me look, will you?"

Mr. Wheeler sprang nimbly to his feet and together they searched over that particular part of the campus. Not a violet showed itself above the close-cropped lawn, nothing but bold-face dandelions.

"Can't you — cut that part out!" he suggested.

"You don't know Miss Rarick," Marcia was genuinely distressed. "If you haven't everything your lesson plan calls for, she just looks at you — and you shrink — and shrivel —"

The wrist watch said three minutes of the hour. "I'll have to take a dandelion root," she announced, "and pass it off for a violet. They won't know the difference." Already her unquenchable spirits were rising. She borrowed Mr. Wheeler's knife and hastily dug up a dandelion. "See! I'll take two or three violet blossoms and leaves" — she took them out of her belt — "attach them to the dandelion root, and wrap my handkerchief around the center as though it were muddy and damp — and there you are!"

"But, see here, they're nothing alike," he protested.

"Oh, we should worry!" said the blithe Miss

Mason. "Thank you for helping me. You can come along if you want to, and see me teach. I'm frightened senseless, anyway, at the Vandyker, so one or two more able-bodied men won't matter."

Mr. Wheeler said he would be delighted to see the dandelion masquerading before the great man. So they hurried up the gravel driveway to the huge training-school building. Marcia pointed out the door where he was to go. "I have to go in another way," she explained; "the righteous from the wicked, you know."

The model primary room was an awe-inspiring place. Eleven student teachers, notebooks in hand, sat by the side walls. Two critic teachers, notebooks in hand, sat by the rear walls. The head supervisor, notebook in hand, walked through the room as though to remind one of the day of judgment. The Capitol City superintendent was there, and two or three lesser lights. Marcia and nine small pupils held the center of the arena after the manner of the early Christian martyrs. Her heart was beating suffocatingly, but she conducted a very creditable little reading class whose lesson was based on a violet plant that was much less modest than it should have been, owing to the fact that its pedal extremities, so to speak, had been grafted from a

110

member of a family noted for its brazen forwardness.

Marcia was a model of the sweet young instructor. Only once did she throw a fleeting glance of roguishness at Mr. Wheeler, to see his mouth lift at the corners in the characteristic way she had liked.

The lesson was over. Every one breathed more naturally. The student teachers and visitors rose to go to chapel exercises. Marcia looked around for Mr. Wheeler, but she did not see him. In the doorway, she turned to look at the Capitol City superintendent, in the hope that he was discussing her with Miss Rarick. He was not so engaged. He was picking up from the floor a dandelion root *alias* a violet.

The sight disturbed her somewhat, but she put the thought of it aside and went on to chapel. Near the Auditorium she came upon a group of senior girls waiting for her. Some days at chapel exercises these girls sat on the front seat and acted virtuously. Some days they sat on the back seat and acted villainously. To-day was apparently one of their pious days, for they filed decorously down the center aisle to the front seat and sang the opening hymn, "Holy, Holy, Holy," as lustily as though they were the original vestal virgins.

The superintendent of the Capitol City

schools, in all his dignity, sat upon the platform with the faculty. After the prayer and announcements, President Wells arose and said, "We have with us to-day the new superintendent of the largest school system in the state." Marcia looked at him, sitting there so calmly. How nice it would be, she thought, to be so undisturbed when you were about to address an audience. President Wells had ceased introducing him, but he did not stir from his chair. Instead, from the semigloom of the back row there was stepping out a tall, clean-cut, alert young man, with keen brown eyes and a strong chin.

All eyes were upon him. Marcia's own, fascinated, alarmed, watched him. The color dropped away from her face, and then surged back like a scarlet tide. From the chaotic jumble of her mind one naked, leering truth stood out. *He* was the superintendent of the Capitol City schools.

Like a kaleidoscope, things she had said to him tumbled about in her brain, forming a nightmare of combinations. With dry lips she whispered to the girl next to her, "Who's the big man — in gray?"

"Supe at Mapleville — only has eight teachers under him — acts like he was Supe of New York City."

The man on the platform was speaking, easily, forcefully. "Earnestness and sincerity form the keystone of the teaching profession." He said a great deal more than that. He said it with fire and enthusiasm. He said he was there to choose teachers, high-grade teachers who had been faithful in their work. Carefulness, attention to details, were things that would be considered. But over and above these was the great fundamental question: What was the spirit of the teacher? What gifts of heart and soul as well as of mind did she come bearing to her task?

Marcia felt stunned, sick. She sat with miserable hot eyes fixed upon her lap. It was over at last. Chapel was out. President Wells and other faculty members had surrounded the speaker. Marcia slipped away from the girls. She attended two classes and got through a noisy boarding-house dinner. She wanted to go home. She wanted to see the family, especially Mother, comfortable and comforting Mother. Katherine would be home for the week-end. She had written to that effect and also that Keith was coming for Sunday.

Marcia did not go to her afternoon classes and she hung a frank "Busy — Keep Out" sign on her door. Then she packed her bag and slipped down to the afternoon train.

At home the family was all excitement over the unexpected arrival. Mother bustled about with happy moisture in her eyes even while she took in the fact that Marcia had something on her mind. When they had finished supper it came out, just as Mother knew it would. They were still sitting about the table — all but Junior, whose urgent business with Runt Perkins and Shorty Marston always found him swallowing his last bites while on the way to the door.

Marcia told them all about it. She spared herself not at all. She had made a fool of herself, she said, and they might as well know it. "The thing that makes me maddest," she informed them, tearfully, "is that I stretched things just to hear him laugh. I made myself out lots worse than I am. He was the sternest-looking man you ever saw, and I *loved* to see the corners of his mouth pull up. It seemed to me he laughed an awful lot," she finished forlornly.

Every one looked sympathetic. Katherine's consolation was, "Marcia, I just can't *imagine* myself talking so glibly to a strange man."

Marcia's contrition was complete. "I can't either, Kathie. I envy you being so cool and sweet and courteous to everybody. Only it *seemed* as though I'd known him a thousand years," she added.

Eleanor's contribution was, "Myself, I think

it was terribly romantic."

Marcia's scorn was withering. "Romantic? *Tragic,* you mean."

Father began a dry, "Well, Marcia, I've always told you you'd run up against —" But as Marcia dabbed a moist roll of handkerchief into her eyes, he finished lamely, "Never mind, honey, I think you can have the third grade here."

Tillie was on the warpath. "There's a law about false pretenses. He ought to be sued. If I was a man I'd trounce the middle of the road with him."

Mother was furtively wiping away a tear or two herself. "Marcia, there's something about you that makes me think of myself when I was a girl." Verily the poet was an inspired philosopher who remarked:

Where can we better be
Than in the bosom of our fam-i-lee?

On Saturday it developed that there were enough young people home for the week-end to get up a fair-sized picnic crowd. Cars were prohibited. Tommie Hickson was to bring in a hayrack so they could all go together.

Mother thought it a fine plan and began bustling preparations for a basket supper. Tillie, whose emotion over Marcia had worn

115

off, was disgruntled to have the Saturday work upset.

"You do spoil them girls, Molly," she volunteered. "Here's Kathie engaged to that Baldridge, and Marcia a grown woman, and even Eleanor getting along. Accordin' to my lights they ought to be hemmin' sheets and piecin' comforts instead a-galavantin' round to picnics."

"Tillie," Mother said calmly, "a very wise poet once wrote about a rich old man who was robbed of all his wealth. The poem ends:

They robbed him not of a golden shred
Of the childish dreams in his wise old head,
And, 'They're welcome to all things, else,'
he said,
When the robbers came to rob him.

I figure you can buy sheets and comforts in any department store, but you can't buy dreams and memories of youth."

"*Pfs!*" Tillie had a special snort that denoted scorn. "You can't eat dreams nor cover your nakedness with memories."

"No," said Mother placidly, "you can't. And when the girls are old, old ladies, the most palatable food won't feed their minds, nor the thickest comforts bring warmth to their hearts."

So they went on working together, side by side, two good old friends who would do anything for each other, but as far apart as the earth and the stars, as far apart as Martha and Mary — a Piecer of Quilts and a Weaver of Dreams.

Tommie Hickson came with the hayrack and two horses, which seemed to share Tillie's scorn for the festivities.

Marcia apparently brightened under the witching spell of the green woods, the pungent, wild smell of the crab-apple blossoms, the sweet, weird call of the mourning doves and the sheen of the silver river. Mother was right. No matter what Fate held in the hollow of her hand, the girls would always have memories left to them.

On the way home, after the manner of youth, the crowd sang. Marcia did not sing. She sat in the end of the hayrack and tried to reason it all out. Since yesterday she felt changed, subdued, unreal. She looked up at the clear, calm face of the yellow-white moon. Why did that hour on the campus seem so set apart from other hours? It was like a little house in the woods. She had come upon it, rested in it for one hour — and gone on again, Must she forever be looking back at the little house by the side of the road?

The crowd was unloaded at the various

homes with merry good nights. The Mason girls found that the rest of the family had gone upstairs for the night. There was a letter on the dining-room mantel. Father had brought it home from the five-o'clock mail. The letter was for Marcia. With fingers that trembled she tore it open and read it. Then she ran upstairs and called "Folks! Everybody! Come here!"

Father and Mother, fully dressed, came to their door. Tillie opened her door cautiously and put out her head; a striped kimono falling away from her long neck gave her the appearance of a curious giraffe. Junior, hearing the noise, came stumbling out of his room. "Listen! It's from *him*." She read aloud:

DEAR MISS MASON: I tried to see you yesterday afternoon but your landlady said you had gone home for over Sunday. I hope you are not taking my talk to heart. Most probably you are not, as your disposition seems to be of a marvelously cheerful and elastic type. And, anyway, what's a dandelion or two between friends?

Have just come from board meeting and have the pleasure of reporting your election. I have placed you in the Lafayette School for next year, the grounds of that building being somewhat overrun with certain yellow weeds. You will no doubt take pleasure in assisting the janitor to eradicate them.

I have just been talking with Keith by 'phone, and if I do not hear from you that it would be inconvenient, I will drop in with him on Sunday and congratulate you in person on the "professional hit" you made with the Capitol City superintendent.

Sincerely,
JOHN R. WHEELER.

Marcia threw out her arms to them all. "Folks!" she said in a little, tense, awe-struck voice, "I *was* born under a lucky star."

"By golly, I believe it!" Father said.

They were all talking at once, after the manner of Masons.

Katherine laughed, "You old fraud, you don't deserve it."

Eleanor's contribution was, "Oh, Marcia, I *adore* a good profile."

Tillie was saying, "My good *land,* you do beat the Dutch!"

Junior, at the close of a prodigious yawn, asked unintelligibly, "Wh'd 'e mean, dandelions?"

Only Mother said nothing. She was looking

119

at the lovely flushed face of her starry-eyed girl and making a little incoherent prayer, "Dear Lord — keep her happy — like that."

The excitement over, they all went back to their rooms.

"I can't help but be glad she got it." Father was pulling off his socks and tenderly regarding his favorite corn. "But it wasn't a very good lesson for her to have it turn out this way."

Mother was immediately on the other side of the argument. "Oh, she's had punishment enough, Father — that scare." Mother brushed her hair for a few moments, and then added, "I must say though, I don't like that dandelion deal; it's too much like deceiving."

Father, with alacrity, veered to the opposite side. "Oh, I don't know," he said cheerfully; "that's what I call good old-fashioned Yankee shrewdness." So they went to bed, arguing amiably, quarreling peaceably as they had done for twenty-six years.

Across the hall, Marcia finished brushing her hair, turned out the light and snapped up the shades. Pale, silvery, golden-white, the moon flooded her slim, youthful figure in its soft, clinging gown. Surreptitiously, deftly, she slipped a large, square envelope under her pillow. Then she said, "Kathie, something tells me I'm going to enjoy teaching with John."

CHAPTER VII

IN WHICH MOTHER RENEWS HER YOUTH

On Sunday Keith Baldridge and John Wheeler came. Like that other Sunday when Keith had first stepped into the family circle, Mother engineered a fine dinner to its palatable end. In the afternoon she and Tillie (the latter protesting that all this foolishness made her sick) put up lunch for the four young people and they took it in Keith's car to the woods.

It was a day of wondrous spring sunshine, the green of new leaves and the song of birds. Every moment was joyous to Marcia and no wood sprite was gayer than she . . . or lovelier. Just before their return home she and John Wheeler sat alone for a few moments on the river bank. The conversation turned on Keith and Katherine.

"He's to be envied," John Wheeler said and added suddenly and seriously. "Until this spring I had about come to the conclusion that the type of love I have dreamed about was going to pass me by. I had almost committed the sin of putting aside that dream and asking a girl I have known a long time to marry me . . . a girl I had merely been fond of as a friend."

"Until this spring!" Marcia thrilled at the magic significance of the words. She was so unspeakably happy that, at home again in the evening, when several of the Springtown young people came in, she veiled her joyousness from any spying eyes by spending most of the evening at the far end of the porch with Nicky Marston. It has been the way of femininity since the world began.

After that Sunday came a box of flowers, with a friendly courteous note . . . and that was apparently the end.

All the spring term Marcia went about trying desperately to conceal that vague little soreness in her heart, a hurt for which she could find no explanation. He sent no other word, made no effort to come back . . . and he had seemed so . . . well, interested in her, Marcia admitted to herself. For the first time in her life a little of the song of joy had gone out of living. It was true, then, there was to be nothing of the little house by the side of the road but a memory.

Mother was unaware that anything was wrong in the scheme of things. In fact she was thinking more about herself than any of the children just then, a most remarkable circumstance. She and Tillie, swathed in mummy-like uniforms, had done the spring house-cleaning. On the evening of the conclusion to this annual orgy of the furniture, Mother accosted Father as he was sitting down by the library table and unfolding the *Journal*.

"Henry, you wait a minute. I want to talk to you about something that has been on my mind all day."

Henry looked up politely, but hung on to his paper.

"This morning I was cleaning out the drawers of that old bureau in the attic and I began reading scraps of letters and looking at the pictures of my old college classmates, and I just got hungry to see them all. I kept thinking about my girlhood with those old chums, and I was so homesick to see them I could *taste* it. Why, if I could hear Nettie Fisher laugh and see Julie Todd's shining, happy face!"

She dropped her mending and turned to her husband.

"Henry, I've a good, big *notion* to plan to go back to Mount Carroll for commencement."

"Why, sure! Why don't you, Mother?"

Henry prepared to plunge into the paper as though the matter were settled, but it seemed Mother had more to say. For twenty-six years Father had been a patient, silent bowlder in the middle of the stream of Mother's chatter. "I want to go back to Mount Carroll and be a girl again. If I could just get with that old crowd it would bring my youth all back, I know. I'd just live it over. Why, Henry, I'd give the price of the trip to have *five* minutes of real girlish thrill —"

"All right, Mother." Father boldly dismissed the subject. "You just plan to go and get your thrill."

In the busy weeks that followed Mother moved in an exalted state of mind, thinking of nothing but plans to leave the family comfortable and the exquisite pleasure before her. She wrote reams of messages to Julie Todd and Nettie Fisher and Myra Breckenridge and a dozen others. To be sure, they had all possessed other names for a quarter of a century, but for old time's sake Mother deigned to use them only on the outside of the envelopes.

There were clothes to be planned. Mother thought Lizzie Beadle could make her something suitable, but Eleanor protested.

"You're not going back there looking *dinky*, Mamma, that's sure."

And Henry added his voice, "That's right, Mother; you doll up."

So Eleanor and Mother journeyed to Capitol City and chose a navy blue tailored suit, and a stunning black and white silk, and a soft gray chiffon gown, "in which she looks *per*fectly Astorbiltish," Eleanor afterward told the assembled family. These, with hat and gloves and a pair of expensive gray suede shoes that hurt her feet, but made them look like a girl's, came to a ghastly sum in three figures, so that Mother felt almost ill when she wrote on the check, "Henry Y. Mason, per Mrs. H. Y. M."

On the evening before the wonderful journey back to the land of youth, Father made his startling announcement. He had been reading quietly in his accustomed place by the library table. Mother, who had just completed her packing by putting pictures of all the family and views of the new house into her bag, came into the library.

"Mother" — Henry put down his magazine — "I've decided to go with you to-morrow and on to Midwestern while you are at Mount Carroll." Father's university was in a state farther east than Mother's Alma Mater. "When you get off at Oxford to change, I'll go right on, and then next Thursday, after commencement, I'll be on the train coming back, and meet you there."

Mother was delighted, reproaching herself severely, in her tender-hearted way, for not having thought of the same thing. Father had attended to business so strictly all these years that this arrangement had not once occurred to her.

"I've been thinking what you said about seeing your old chums, and, by George! I'd enjoy it, too," Henry went on. "I can't think of anything more pleasurable than meeting Slim Reed and the Benson boys, and old Jim Baker."

So Father got his hat and went back to the bank to attend to some business; for with that nonchalant way a man has of throwing a clean collar into a grip preparatory to a long journey there was nothing for him to do at home.

Kind-hearted Mother's cup of joy was bubbling over. Happy moisture stood in her eyes as she got out Father's things. How well he deserved the trip!

Hurrying back into the library to get a late magazine for him to take along, her eyes fell upon the one he had just been reading. It was the *Midwestern University Alumnus*. Smiling, Mother picked it up. Under the news from Father's class there were a couple of commonplace items. Her eyes wandered on. Under it there was a clever call for a reunion of the next class signed by the secretary, Laura Drew Westerman. Mother sat down heavily, and the Thing, after a long hibernating period, awoke and raised its scaly head.

Now, there is in the life of every married woman a faint, far-away, ghostly personage known as the Old Girl. Just how much they had meant to each other, Mother had never known. She did know that every spring and fall for twenty-six years she had cleaned out a box which contained, among other trinkets, an autograph album and a copy of *Lucile* and a picture of a dark-eyed girl in a ridiculously big-sleeved dress, all marked "To Henry from Laura." Laura Drew was Henry's old girl.

So from this lack of knowledge and the instinct inherited from primal woman had been hatched a little slimy creature, so unworthy of Mother that she had refused to call it by its real name. That had been years ago. With the coming of children and the passing of years, the Thing had shriveled up, both from lack of nourishment and because Mother laughed at it. A Thing like that cannot live in the white light of humor. But now, quite stunned by the sudden surprise that the Thing was alive, she could only listen passively to what it was saying:

"So! even though he has been kind and loving and good and true to you," It said tragically, for It loves to be tragic, *"across the years she has called to him."*

On the train the next day, Mother steeled herself to venture, quite casually: "I saw by your *Alumnus* last night that Laura Drew is to be there."

"Yes, I saw that, too," Father said simply, and the subject was dropped.

On the station platform at Oxford, Mother clung to Father's arm for just a second, he seemed so boyish and enthusiastic. She stood for several minutes by the side of her bags watching the train curve around the bend of the bluff, carrying Father down the road to youth — and Laura Drew.

Then, with characteristic good sense, she determined to put the thought completely out of her mind and devote herself to the resurrection of her own youth. So she walked energetically into the station, spread a paper on the dusty bench, and sat down. Her feet hurt her, but the trim girlish appearance of the gray suede shoes peeping out from under the smart suit was full compensation for all earthly ills.

A little gray-haired, washed-out woman in an out-of-date, limpsy suit was wandering aimlessly around the room. In the course of her ramblings she confronted Mother with a question concerning the train to Mount Carroll. Mother, in turn, interrogated the woman. *It was Julie!* Julie Todd, whose round, happy face Mother had crossed two states to see. Poor Mother!

After the first shock, she drew Julie down beside her on the bench and the two visited until their train came. Julie had no permanent home. Her husband, it seemed, had been unfortunate, first in losing the money his father had left him, and then in having his ability underestimated by a dozen or so employers. He was working just now for a dairyman — it was very hard on him, though — out in all sorts of weather.

There were seven children, unusually smart, too, but their father's bad luck seemed to shadow them. Joe, now, had been in the army, and had left camp for a little while — he had fully intended to go back; but the officers were very disagreeable and unjust about it. And on and on through an endless tale of grievances.

It was late afternoon when the train arrived at Mount Carroll. The station was a mass of moving students, class colors, arriving parents and old grads. Mother's spirits were high.

Em met them and took them to her pretty bungalow on College Hill. Em had never married. She was Miss Emmeline Livingston, head of the English Department, and she talked with the same pure diction to be found in Boswell's *Life of Johnson*. Also, she was an ardent follower of a new cult which had for its main idea, as nearly as Mother could ascertain, the conviction that if you lost your money or your appetite or your reputation, you had a perfect right to make yourself believe that there had been chaos where there should have been cosmos.

Nettie Fisher and Myra Breckenridge had arrived that morning, and were there to greet Mother and Julie Todd. Nettie Fisher was a widow, beautifully gowned in black. She had enormous wealth; but the broken body of her only boy lay under the poppies in a Flanders field, and she had come to meet these girlhood friends to try and find surcease for the ache that never stopped.

Myra Breckenridge had no children, dead or living. Her sole claims to distinction seemed to be that she was the champion woman bridge-player of her city, and that her bulldog had taken the blue ribbon for two consecutive years. She wore a slim, flame-colored dress cut on sixteen-year-old lines. Her fight with Time had been persistent, as shown by the array of weapons on her dressing table. But Time was beginning to fight with his back to the wall.

They made an incongruous little group, as far apart now as the stars and the seas; but it had not evidenced itself to Mother, who, with blind loyalty, told herself during dinner that a noticeable stiffness among them would soon wear off.

After dinner, Mother unpacked her bags and hung the pretty gowns in a cedar closet. But the photographs that had been packed with happy anticipation she left in the bag. It would be poor taste to display the views of her cherished sun-parlor and fireplace and mahogany stairway to poor Julie, who had no home. It would be cruel to flaunt the photographs of all those lovely daughters and sturdy sons before Nettie, whose only boy had thrown down the flaming torch. So Mother closed the bag and went downstairs to meet the three boys of the old class who had come to call.

One of the boys was a fat judge, with a shining, bald head and a shining, round face behind shining, round tortoise-shell glasses. One was a small, wrinkled, dapper dry-goods merchant. And one was a tall doctor with a Van Dyke beard. This completed the reunion of the class.

There were numberless seats and chairs on the roomy porch of the bungalow, and it was there that they all sat down. The hour that followed was not an unqualified success. The reunion appeared not to be living up to its expectations. The old crowd was nothing but a group of middle-aged people who were politely discussing orthopedic hospitals and the reconstruction of Rheims. Occasionally, some one referred with forced jocularity to a crowd of jolly young folks they had once known. Ah, well! after all, you can't recapture youth by trying to throw salt on its tail.

Sensing that things were lagging, Mother proposed that they walk up to the old school, with Em to show them around. They found a dozen unfamiliar buildings, an elaborate new home for the president, and a strange campanile pointing its finger, obelisk like, to the blue sky. Only the green-sloping campus smiled gently at them like a kind old mother whose sweet face welcomed them home.

On Monday they attended the literary society's pageant. As the slowly moving lines of brilliantly costumed girls came into view, Mother's heart was throbbing in time to the notes of the bugle. With shining eyes she turned to the little widow.

"Nettie," she said solemnly, "we girls *started* this parade day."

"I know it. We all had big white tissue paper hats with pink roses on them —"

"And we stole the Beta's stuffed monkey so they wouldn't have a mascot —"

"And got up at four o'clock to pick clovers for the chain."

They had made the first chain, and now, gray haired, they were standing on tiptoe at the edge of the crowd trying to catch a glimpse of the lithe, radiant, marching girls — eternal youth forever winding in and out under the shimmering leaves of the old oaks!

It was like that for three days. They seemed always to be on the outskirts of things, looking on. For three days they went everywhere together — class plays, receptions, ball games, musicals — this little lost flock of sheep. For three days Mother exerted herself to the utmost to catch one glimpse of the lost youth of these men and women. Apparently they saw everything with mature vision, measured everything by the standard of a half-century's experience.

On the evening of the last day Mother gave up. She was through, she thought, as they all sat together on the porch. There was to be a concert by the united musical organizations, and the old crowd was ready to go and sit sedately through the last session. Very well, thought Mother, as she chatted and rocked, she would try no more. They were hopelessly, irrevocably middle-aged. She was convinced at last, disillusioned, she told herself. You can never, never recapture youth.

Then, quite gradually, so that no one knew just how it began, there came a change. Some one said, "Remember, Myra, the night that red-headed Philomathian came to call on you, and we girls tied a picture of your home beau on a string and let it down through the stove-pipe hole into his lap?"

And some one else said, "Remember, Em, the time you had to read Hamlet's part in 'Shake' class and Professor Browning criticized you so severely, and then said, 'Now you may continue,' and you read in a loud voice, 'Well said, you old mole'?"

And the doctor said, "Remember, Jim, the note you pinned on your laundry to the wash-lady:

If all the socks I've sent to thee
Should be delivered home to me,
Ah, well! the bureau would not hold
So many socks as there would be,
If all my socks came home to me?"

And before they were aware, they were going off into gales of laughter.

It came time for the concert, but no one suggested starting. Each succeeding anecdote heightened the merriment so that the under-grads streaming by said patronizingly, "Pipe the old duffers!"

"Remember, boys, the Hallowe'en we girls hid from you, and you had to furnish the sup-

134

per because you didn't find us by nine o'clock?"

They all began talking at once about it, the men protesting that the girls had come out from the hiding place before nine.

"If you girls hadn't nigged on the time, we'd have found you," the men were arguing. There was a perfect bedlam of voices. Youth, which up to this time had eluded them, had slipped, slyly, unbidden, into their midst. Mother was thrilling to her finger tips.

"It was a night almost as warm as this," the judge said, "and the moon was as gorgeous as it is to-night."

Mother, in the stunning black and white silk, jumped to her feet.

"Let's do it again!" she cried with an impulsive sweep of her hands. "To-night! It's the nearest to youth we'll ever come in our whole lives." She turned to the men on the steps. "The rules are the same, boys. Give us fifteen minutes' start, and if you can't find us by nine, we'll come back here, and you'll buy the supper. If you find us, we'll buy it. Come on, girls."

As Joan of Arc may have led her armies, so Mother's power over the others seemed to hold. In a wave of excitement, they rose to her bidding. Light of foot, laughing, the five women hurried across one corner of the campus. In the shadow of the oaks Mother stopped them.

"Is the same house still standing?" she asked breathlessly of Em.

"Yes, but others are built up around it now."

"Come on, then!" With unerring feet, down to the same house where they had hidden twenty-nine years before, Mother led them.

"What if some one sees us?" giggled Nettie.

"We should worry!" said the head of the English Department, which was really the most remarkable thing that happened that night.

There it was — a house no longer new — but still standing, and as dark as the others near it. Evidently the occupants had gone to the concert. By the light of the moon they could see its high cellar windows, still yawning foolishly open, waiting for them, just as it had waited before.

Against the window they placed a sloping board and climbed slowly up, one by one. Em went first, then Myra, and Nettie, and Julie, and, last, Mother. At least, Mother's intentions were good. The window was about eighteen by twenty; and Mother, quite eighteen by twenty herself, stuck halfway in and halfway out. Up the street they could hear the old whistle — the boys calling to each other.

Laughing hysterically, tugging desperately at her, the other four, after strenuous labor, pulled Mother down into the cellar, where, groping around in the dark, she found the cellar stairs and sat down. They were all shaking with laughter spasms, that kind of digestion-aiding laughter which comes less often in the ratio of the number of years you are away from youth.

For some time, whispering and giggling nervously and saying "Sh!" constantly to each other, they sat in the black cellar.

Suddenly, an electric light snapped on over Mother's head and the door above her opened. "What are you doing in my cellar?" snarled a voice as gruff as the biggest bear's in "Goldilocks."

The giggling died as suddenly as though it had been chloroformed.

Cold as ice, Mother rose and faced the darkness above her. Then she said with all her Woman's Club dignity — which is a special de luxe brand of dignity — "If you will allow us to come up there, I think we can make a very satisfactory explanation."

"You can explain to the town marshal," answered the sour voice, and the owner of it slammed the door.

They sat down dismally and waited. They heard the telephone ring and then the wooden shutter of the cellar window was banged down and fastened.

"He needn't have done *that*," Mother said stiffly. It is claimed that housebreakers are often sensitive about their honor.

During the long wait every fiber of Mother's brain concentrated on one word — *disgrace*. If the papers got hold of it! Even if they wrote it up as a joke! Imagine — to be written up as a joke at fifty-two!

There were footsteps overhead, and then the gruff voice, "Come up out of there now!"

Slowly they filed up the narrow dark stairs. Mother went first. As she had led them into this sickening dilemma, so would she be the first to face the music.

"May we have some lights?" she asked frigidly.

"Certainly."

Lights were turned on. Three men stood there: A fat one with tortoise-shell glasses; a little, wrinkled, dapper one, and a tall one with a Van Dyke beard — all fiery red from silent convulsions brought on by ingrowing laughter. As the women filed in, the pent-up laughter rolled forth from the men in shrieks and howls. Then the shouting and the tumult died, for Nettie and Julie were smothering the fat one with some one's sofa pillows, Myra and Em were taking care of the bearded one, and Mother was shaking the little one, while he motioned feebly with his hands that he was ready for peace.

"Kamarad!" gasped the fat judge when he could get his breath. "Anyway, you'll admit we were speaking the truth when we said we could have found you."

"Now let's dig out," said the doctor, whose respiratory organs were again working, "before the folks that own this house come home from the concert and send us all up."

Breaking out into hilarious laughter at intervals, they walked down to the store at the foot of the hill, and there the girls bought a lunch to make angels weep. It consisted of buns, bananas, wienies, chocolate candy, and dill pickles.

Across pastures, crawling under barb-wire fences, went the cavalcade, to build a bonfire down by old Salt Creek. Gone were the years and the family ties. Forgotten were the hours of failure and the hours of triumph. They were the old crowd singing, "Solomon Levi." Youth was in their midst. And the moon, bored to the point of *ennui*, at the countless hordes of students it had seen roasting wienies in that identical spot, brightened at the novel sight of the old duffers taking hold of hands while they sang and danced around the huge fire.

As chimes from the campanile striking twelve came faintly through the night, youth suddenly dropped her festive garments and fled, a Cinderella that could not stay.

The little straggling procession started soberly back across the meadow. Julie's rheumatism was beginning to manifest itself. The head of the English Department was painfully aware that in the place where she had stowed that awful collection of indigestibles there was chaos where there should have been cosmos. Far, far behind the others came the judge and Mother; not from any sentimental memory of their past friendship, but because, being the possessors of too, too solid flesh, they were frankly puffed-out.

Father swung off the steps of the train at Oxford and took Mother's bags.

"Well, did you get your thrill, Mother?"

"I most certainly did." Mother was smiling to herself.

They walked down the Pullman to Father's section, which he had chosen with careful regard to Mother's comfort.

"And you — did you have a good time?" Mother questioned when they were seating themselves.

"Fine — just fine!" Father was enthusiasm personified.

A quick little tug at Mother's heart reminded her that the Thing was still alive.

"Were there many of your old classmates back?" she parried, giving herself time to bring out the real question.

"Two, just two." Father was glowing at the happy memory of some unuttered thing. "Just old Jim Baker and I. Jim's kind of down and out — works around the University Cafeteria."

"Was — ?" It was coming. Mother braced herself. "Was Laura Drew there?"

"Yes." Father's face shone with the light of unspoken pleasure. "Yes, she was there."

The Thing seemed to bite at Mother's throat and wrap a strangling tail around her heart. With the pleasure with which we turn the knife in our wounds, she asked in a tense little voice:

"Is she — does she seem the same?"

Father drew his rapt gaze from some faraway vision to look at Mother.

"The same?" he repeated, a trifle dazed. Then he said cheerfully, "Why — maybe — I don't know. I didn't see her."

"Didn't *see* her?"

"No. I didn't see much of anybody." Father grew confidential. "The fact is, old Jim Baker and I played checkers 'most all the time for the three days. He got off every morning at eleven and we'd go around to his room. By

George! It was nip and tuck for two days. But the last day — *I beat him.*"

"*Checkers!*" Mother breathed but the one word, but the ingredients of which it was composed were incredulity, disgust and merriment.

Then she laughed, a bubbling, deliciously girlish laugh, and the Thing relaxed its hold on her heart, turned up its toes, and died.

Surreptitiously, Mother reached down and pulled off the expensive suede shoes. "Now," she announced, "there's one grateful pair of feet in the world."

Then she fixed herself for the long ride to the West. "Henry," she laid a plump hand on Father's arm, "you are *such* a comfort to me. Won't it be nice to get home and settle down to being middle-aged folks?"

CHAPTER VIII

BOB AND MABEL MEET TRAGEDY

After Mother's return from Mount Carroll the family slipped into the routine occasioned by the hot days of the summer. Katherine, in that domestic way of hers, took up the daily work easily. Eleanor, sunburned almost beyond repair by tennis, was as active as a swallow. Junior, with all of the inventive genius of an imitation Edison and the energy of a tractor engine, made the days dangerous to the neighborhood. Marcia — ! With her all-seeing eye Mother had detected that vague little soreness that her gayest daughter was harboring, and in that sympathetic way which was a part of her, she felt as hurt as Marcia. Wisely she said nothing. In September Marcia would be going to Capitol City. She would see John Wheeler there. If it was to be, thought Mother, the friendship would pick up again.

And two blocks away from the Masons' there was a little tragedy going on.

It seems almost cruel to take advantage of

143

the fact that in the household of Bob and Mabel domestic affairs were at their lowest ebb. But on this hot summer day, the sweltering sun at high noon, the tide had gone out. The magic waves that made of the little house an enchanting fairy castle with towers and turrets of arabesque had felt the urge of some vagrant moon and receded. And behold! On the sands stood only a bungalow, very tiny, rather dirty, and wholly upset.

For the woman who does her own work, there is something about noon, high noon in summer, to try the patience of a saint. That particular time of day may mean nothing to the proportion of femininity that steps out of limousines and walks nonchalantly into palm-bordered, electric-cooled tea-rooms for luncheon. But for that vast proportion that does its own work there is no time so trying: the scorching sun, the warm kitchen, the cooking dinner, the crying baby, the hungry man coming home. It takes the courage of an Amazon and the sweetness of St. Cecilia to go unscathed through high noon of a hot summer day.

And Mabel seemed to have lost both of these requisites. It was Thursday and she had been trying to finish an ironing that, having hung over from Tuesday, seemed endless. Betty had needed an unusual amount of attention. Dirty dishes stood gloomily in the sink. There were little rolling, feathery wisps of dust on the hard-wood floors. A bunch of faded sweet peas stood in a cut-glass vase like a withered old woman in a satin dress. The whole house had that forlorn, untidy look it acquires when the director drops her baton and all the instruments go wrong.

Mabel was tired, with a tiredness that seemed of the spirit as well as the body. The work that once she had so joyed in the doing, seemed, during the last few weeks, to have taken upon itself the form of a Machiavellian monster, a horn-and-claw nightmare that leered at her and would not give her peace.

It was time for Bob to come. She put her ironing board away and listlessly set the table. She did not want anything to eat, but she laid a plate for herself.

Bob came in, glanced at the tumbled-looking house and, in silence, went out to take water to the chickens. When he returned, Mabel put on the boiled potatoes, unmashed, the stewed tomatoes, some inferior dried beef, and bread that plainly said, "Darling, I am growing old." Then, hastily, she opened a can of cherries. To open canned fruit when there were fresh raspberries out on the bushes! But she had not had time to pick them.

It was not a nice meal. No one knew it better than Mabel.

It was not a successful affair from any standpoint — edible, artistic, or conversational. Bob was not unpleasant. Nor was he pleasant. He was merely a silent, stolid fixture, a human machine that sat and automatically worked its jaws.

Betty pounded her mug on the shelf of her high chair and, with that delicate choice of opportune moments displayed by our offspring, began to bawl vigorously for apparently no reason at all, stiffening and straining her fat little stomach against the shelf until it nearly gave way.

"What ails that kid?" Bob's speech broke quarantine. "Can't you do anything with her?" There is nothing so aggravating to tired nerves as the implication from a paternal parent that "a kid" belongs only to its mother.

Mabel rose stiffly and took the offending culprit, who lunged up and down in her arms with all the agility of an animated pump handle. Nor did she go back to the table. She stayed in the bedroom, trying to subdue the human hurricane. She heard Bob push back his chair. Then he called briefly, "Won't be home to supper. After the bank closes, I'm going over to Greenwood with Jim Hartzell and Nicky Marston."

146

Mabel's answer was an indistinguishable monosyllable. Then the front door slammed.

There was a street fair at Greenwood, a horrid, common thing with merry-go-rounds and confetti and dancing girls. A wave of disgust went over her that Bob should care to go. Jim and Nicky were not married. If they chose to spend their time that way, no one was especially concerned. But Bob!

Mabel came out of the bedroom with Betty, who, with the changeableness of a summer squall, had turned into an angelic little creature, and was voluntarily bestowing damp kisses on her mother's cheek.

Mabel looked mechanically at the clock. It was only twelve-thirty-five, and Bob was not due at the bank until one-fifteen. He had gone because home was not pleasant. She did not blame him. She blamed only herself. But she was so fagged!

She started to clear off the table, but a nausea seized her, a sickening lassitude that seemed both mental and physical.

She went back into her bedroom and dropped down on the bed, the bed that was not made. So this was the way Destiny was going to treat them? Squeeze them mercilessly in the hollow of its hand? Make of their family life a flat, monotonous thing, unlovely and bitter?

Betty, who had pulled herself up by the cedar chest on fat, wobbly legs, sat back again so hard that she cried. Under like circumstances Mabel had always run to her with little endearing words of comfort. Now she only lay watching the little thing's tears in a curious, detached sort of way.

The hot sun shone in through the windows. From the bed she could see the dining-room table with the dirty dishes and the remains of the untempting meal. The room looked strange to her, and hostile, like an alienated friend with malice on his face. It was hard to realize that it was the same room that had sheltered love, when love was a throbbing, pulsing thing. Memories of old incidents, things Bob had said and done, came to her with poignant contrast to the dragging days of this miserable summer. It is the saddest thing of all when the tide goes out, that on the dreary beach lie the broken, bleaching bones of all the dear things-that-have-been.

If this were a photoplay, there would now be flashed on the screen: "In the meantime —" and you would behold Mother in a light afternoon dress with a parasol in her hand, coming down the front steps of the Mason home. A close-up would show the kind face that no one in the audience would call handsome, and the graying hair, and the dainty white surplice of her dress.

You would be told that she was on her way to attend a Foreign Missionary meeting, and very soon afterward you would see her going down the basement steps of a dignified but benignant-looking church.

What you would not be told, however, is the fact that the parasol was brand-new, for of course all movie parasols are new. On such a slight detail hung the change in Mother's afternoon plans, for she did not at any time go down the steps of the benignant-looking church. Which is the difference between a flesh-and-blood mother and a celluloid one.

On the corner she stopped, realizing that she was early, a very unusual circumstance, for she usually went rushing in breathless to everything. With as childish a reason for going around to Mabel's as the showing of her new black-and-white-silk parasol to her daughter-in-law, Mother turned up the side street.

There were two ways to go to Mabel's. The morning way was up through the alley, across a street and down Mabel's alley. The afternoon way was up Washington Street one block and down Locust another block. Seeing it was afternoon and Mother had on her lavender pinstripe and an amethyst brooch, to say nothing of the new parasol, she naturally took the way of the sidewalk.

Partly because she felt well dressed and partly because she was entirely at peace with the world, Mother's thoughts were very pleasant ones. They dwelt on nothing very long or very definitely, but jumped about like a little girl with a skipping rope. She thought of her part in the missionary lesson, to report the recent high-caste conversions in Mesopotamia. Mother was a little vague as to where Mesopotamia was, but, as the other good ladies would be equally as vague, it did not worry her. She thought of the way a slight breeze had unexpectedly sprung up, and how pretty Mrs. Marston's geranium boxes were, and how nice it was that the chicken pox sign was gone from the Thompson house, and how attractive Bob's and Mabel's bungalow looked down the street.

Before Mother arrives there, it might be well to insert something of Bob's and Mabel's romance which, paradoxically, had not seemed romantic to any one but themselves. It was only the outrageously frank Marcia, however, who had said it out loud: "Believe *me,* if I ever have a serious affair, I pray the gods it won't be with some one I've played 'run-sheep-run' and 'steal-sticks' with all my life." This, of course, had been several years before.

"Well, they certainly ought to know each other," Father had remarked cheerfully.

"I should say *so*," Marcia had agreed. "Bob was present when Mabel knocked out her first loose tooth, and Mabel has seen Bob with dirty rags tied on his stubbed toes, and *isn't* that romantic?"

No, there had been nothing highly exciting about Bob's courtship. Mabel had played "ante-over" in the neighborhood crowd, a quiet little girl with thick, ashy-light hair and a sprinkle of freckles across a nose that followed literally the motto "Look up — not down."

She was an only child, fatherless at ten. Her mother, with that tigerlike ferocity with which a delicate woman will sometimes get up and attack life for the sake of her offspring, had worked at sewing early and late that her daughter might have schooling.

Mabel had grown from a quiet little girl into a demure young lady, her ashy hair wound round her head in thick braids, her nose still uptilted, although the freckles, ashamed of their existence, had miraculously vanished into the background. No one could call her pretty, but she was gentle mannered, sweet of face, and the possessor of a certain shy drollness that was very attractive to those who knew her well. "And she certainly does know how to keep house," Mother would always say.

Bob, finishing high school, had gone away to college. There had been great things expected of him in the Mason household, for he was the apple of Mother's eye. From the moment he was placed, red and colicky, in her arms, and she noted the wonderful shape of his head, Mother had had visions of him jauntily upholstering the Presidential chair.

Here's to the mothers who hang above cradles and foresee the wonderful destinies of the little mites of humanity who lie there sleeping! May they continue, down the ages, to believe with roseate confidence that they have given birth to the brilliant leaders of the world's thought, instead of blundering draymen, mediocre clerks, and grumbling icemen.

Yes, Bob was to do wonderful things. He was first to finish his collegiate work, and then, because there are many footprints made by lawyers' boots in the dust of the Presidential road, he was to study the late Mr. Blackstone. Mother used to dream how he would come back to Springtown, his every move noted by a group of anxious reporters, back to eat some of Mother's cooking. To be sure, it had turned out that he came back for Mother's cooking, but it was from only two blocks away.

During Bob's college course, Mabel's mother had died, quite unexpectedly, fighting to the last, but partially resigned because her girl was going to marry as good a boy as Bob Mason. Bob had come home and stated definitely that he was through school; that he was going in the bank with Father and earn a home for Mabel. Father and Mother had talked with him, attempting to dissuade him, and trying to think of some satisfactory arrangement for Mabel while he went on to school, but he had been obstinate. Mother had even gone so far as to suggest that he was young and perhaps there would some time be another girl — ? Bob had given her a penetrating look, and said quietly, "You know that isn't so, Mother!" And Mother, remembering the tenacity with which he had always clung to his boyhood decisions, had known it was not true.

So Bob had gone in the bank, and he and his only sweetheart were married. Mother had sighed and put away her dreams along with Bob's baby shoes, over which she shed a few sentimental tears every spring and fall when she cleaned the attic bureau. Then, mother-like, she had figuratively dusted the Presidential chair for Junior.

Mother arrived at the bungalow and went

up the front steps, placing, as she passed, an investigating finger in the fern box. Dry as a bone, she thought!

The porch was dusty, the front door locked. Through the small-paned glass she could see Betty creeping hurriedly toward her like a little dog with its head in the air.

"Where's Mamma?" Mother called.

"Da-ja-schpee!" Betty blubbered, putting a soiled little fist out to Grandma.

Mabel came to the front door and let Mother in. She smiled, but it was a soulless, shadowy ghost of a smile. "Come in, Mother, I'm ashamed of the way I look. I haven't even cleared off my — I ought to have swept the — I —" She was making futile little lunges toward spools and wooly animals on the floor.

With that instinct that would have made of her an able Pinkerton or Burns assistant, Mother knew that something was radically wrong. It was in the atmosphere. Almost she could smell it.

But she only said cheerfully, "Oh, don't mind *me!* I guess you can't tell *me* how hard it is to keep things up with a baby."

Mabel sat down on the davenport, the dusty davenport, a taut little figure with clenched fists. "I was ironing — and things piled up so — and Betty seemed to take so much care — and —" It went swiftly through her mind that she couldn't even *talk* about anything but that work.

"Then just sit still and rest a few minutes before I go on," Mother said comfortably. She unearthed from somewhere about her ample person a crochet needle and thread, and settled back in her chair.

"It's awful hot weather to do all your work and take care of the baby. I know just how you feel." Mother had meant to say something soothing, but it had the effect of bringing swift tears to Mabel's eyes.

"I'd get along better if I could ever catch up," she said in a quavery voice. "I'm not well — I — I'll be all right after a while —" She turned her head from Mother. She was not crying but her voice was at the breaking point.

Mother looked keenly at her for a moment, and then asked her a gentle question, to which Mabel nodded her head and burst weakly into a flood of tears.

"Why, Mabel dear, you should have told me before."

"I didn't want to — I — Oh, Mother, Betty is *so* little yet, but even then I wouldn't care if — if Bob was all right about it."

"Bob?" Mother questioned.

"Yes." The little figure on the big davenport was trying to control its sobs. "He's never even mentioned it . . . since the day I told him . . . and all he said that time was just — 'Oh, my g-good gosh!' "

Mother's sense of humor, like the poor, she always had with her. It did sound funny, but she would as soon have thought of laughing at a blind man's affliction as at Mabel.

"I think about it so much," the younger mother went on. "I can't tell you how I feel that he doesn't like it . . . sort of *degraded!* And the worst part of it is I'll make the little thing moody and cross by my attitude."

"Oh, *shoot!*" Mother was definitely concise. "There's not the slightest thing in *that.* If ever I was gloomy and down-at-the-mouth in my life, it was before Marcia was born. Just think, Mabel, she was my third, all mere babies, and I supposed, of course, Marcia would be a cross, moody child, and, instead, you know yourself that if Marcia were lost in an African jungle, she'd manage to have fun with the parrots and orang-outangs."

Mabel gave a faint, wan smile. Mother Mason was certainly a comforting confessor.

"I've tried to keep pleasant," Mabel went on. "You don't know *how* I've tried. I have that verse pinned up on my dresser, about

*The man worth while is the man who can
    smile,*
When everything goes dead wrong."

"Take it down," Mother said cheerfully. "If there's a verse in the world that has been worked overtime, it's that one. I can't think of anything more inane than to smile when everything goes dead wrong, unless it is to cry when everything is passably right. That verse always seemed to me to be a surface sort of affair. Take it down and substitute 'I will lift up mine eyes unto the hills from whence cometh my help.' *That* goes to the heart of things — when you feel *that* strength, then the dead-wrong things begin to miraculously right themselves."

Mother paused to pick out a crochet stitch and then went on: "About Bob, I must say that doesn't seem real nice of him, but he's like his father. He's all Mason. And Henry can keep still about things the longest of any one I ever knew. *I* want to say everything right out and get it over. Marcia is like me, and so's Junior. Katherine and Eleanor are partially like their father, but Bob's just *all* Mason. Henry used to worry me terribly when we were first married. I've had him come home to dinner and sit and eat — and say nothing much — until I wanted to scream.

157

I thought he was brooding about something, or that the dinner was disgusting him, or that he was wishing he had married his old girl." Mother gave a chuckle. "And I had spells of being downright miserable, until I came to the conclusion that he would never change, and that I couldn't make him talk freely about things any more than he could stop my continual chatter."

Mother looked up with a deprecatory smile. "Far be it from me, Mabel, to preach. I never could stand some old woman coming in and handing out free advice. We all have to work out our own salvation. As my Scotch mother used to say, 'Every Jennie has a-muckle to do wi' her own Jockie.' But I want you to know that I've been through all this. We're all inclined to think we have a monopoly on each new sensation that comes to us, that it's our own particular little grievance. But every feeling and every thought you may have now has probably been felt and thought by mothers from the time the world began. Fundamentally, you and Bob are no different from Isaac and Rebekah. Just keep as cheerful as you consistently can, and hang onto your faith that these minor ups and downs make not a whit of difference with the great love you bear each other."

Mother rolled up her crochet work.

"There! I usually charge fifty cents for this lecture, but seeing it's *you* it will only be a quarter." She went off into such a gay little laugh that Mabel gave a watery imitation of it.

Mother turned up the sheer lavender skirt around her waist and pinned it with a capable looking safety-pin. So far as Mother was concerned, every member of the Springtown missionary auxiliary could die in total ignorance of there ever having been a high-caste convert in Mesopotamia.

"Now, I have a little plan. It popped into my head ready to spring out full-sized, like Minerva or Diana, or whoever it was that did that little acrobatic stunt." Having raised a household of young folks, Mother sometimes used shocking language. "Anyway, it's a good plan. What *you* need is a change. You're coming to my house to visit me, until — let's see — next Tuesday evening. That will be five days in which you are not to turn your hand, either to work or look after Betty. You pack everything you need, for if you forget anything you can't come back after it any more than if you had gone on a trip a hundred miles from here."

"Oh, Mother, there are the chickens!" Mabel protested.

"We'll tell the little McCabe boy he can

have the eggs for looking after them."

"And eggs are *so* high!"

"Not as high as nerves," Mother retorted. She was pinning one of Mabel's bungalow aprons around her ample waist, using the sleeves for strings.

Mabel protested vehemently, but Mother was firm. "You go take a hot bath," she told her. "There's nothing like a bath for troubles."

"But I can't leave the house like this."

"Oh, yes, you can." Mother was pleasantly certain of that. "I'll wash the dishes, and then we'll just close the door on everything; and next Wednesday morning you can go to work again to your heart's content."

Mother picked up Betty and put her in the high chair, and from three potatoes and some toothpicks made her a fat horse and a crooked-necked cow.

In the late afternoon Mother and Mabel strolled toward the Mason home with Betty in the cab, a clean Betty, hugging a crooked-necked potato cow to her bosom.

When Father came home from the bank Mother told him to take the car and go after Betty's crib. Father went off as he was told. He was one of those men who have learned to have implicit faith in their wives' management. If Mother had said, "Henry, take this pail and bring me some milk from the Milky Way," he would have unthinkingly reached for the bucket.

It seemed nice to be with Bob's fun-loving family. And better still, it seemed heavenly not to have anything to do. They were all out on the big porch when Bob came from Greenwood, came with the information that he had had a bum supper and been to a punk show. When the five-day visit was explained to him, he said, "Good enough! We've been living on short rations for three weeks."

Mabel, who would have had to fight to keep back the tears at such a statement earlier in the day, fortified now by Mother's talk, laughed surprisingly with the others when Mother said, "It has probably been a heap sight better than you deserved, son."

After all, there are only about seventy waking hours in five days, so the time was not long. Under Mother's stern edict, Mabel did not so much as see the kitchen. With shameless regularity Mother surreptitiously hired Eleanor and Junior to take turns in caring for Betty. There were good meals, of which Mabel partook with growing appetite, and there were company and music, and a great deal of nonsensical conversation.

On Tuesday afternoon, just before the supper hour, Bob and Mabel went home, accompanied by a market basket in which Mother had packed some things for their supper.

Mabel got out of the car and carried Betty up the front walk. The fern boxes dripped cool moisture. The porch was clean. The windows were shining. Bob unlocked the door, and he and his father carried Betty's little white enameled bed into the house.

Mabel stepped into the living room and looked about her. There was not a flicker of dust in sight. Everything shone. "Tillie!" she thought. Mother had sent Tillie to help her "catch up." She recalled Mother's vague, "Oh, Tillie went away for the day."

She could not know, of course, that when Mother explained matters to Tillie, and asked her to go over and do up the work for Mabel, Tillie had sniffed and remarked in her usual agreeable manner, "Huh! I guess this gettin' married ain't what it's cracked up to be. There's thorns a-plenty in it, I'm thinkin'."

"Yes, Tillie," Mother had said placidly, "there are." And then she had smiled a little as she finished the quotation to herself, " 'But ain't the roses sweet?' "

Mabel passed on to the dining room. Yes, there was the ultimate proof that Tillie had been there. The cut-glass wedding vase stood on the table. In it was one of Tillie's hodge-podge bouquets, consisting of a large yellow marigold, two scarlet poppies, some stiff zinnias of a dull magenta color and a handful of variegated verbenas. A more inartistic combination could scarcely be conceived, but to Mabel it was the gift *with* the giver, and it was not bare.

Father, with a final tousling of Betty, went away.

Now is the time, if this were a model story and not just the simple, unadorned chronicles of an ordinary American family, that Bob would take Mabel in his arms and say, "Home again, dear heart."

He did nothing of the kind. He said, "I'll bet there are enough raspberries to make a mess for supper."

So he took a pan and went whistling out to the back yard and Mabel took off her hat and hung it in the closet. Then she went into the kitchen, her shining, sweet-smelling, fascinating kitchen, and unpacked the basket that Mother had sent. She got out fresh linen and set the dining table. She was glad to be home again in her sweet, clean home, where everything was her own. She touched the dishes lovingly as she placed the buns and the cold sliced meat and the sponge cake on the table. Betty, who had found an old battered doll, was sitting quietly in the corner and industriously endeavoring to pick its one eye out.

After a while Bob came in with the berries. "There's enough for a pie, too, Mabel," he called to her.

"Good! I'll make one to-morrow. I'm just *aching* to bake something again. I believe I'll make cookies, too, cream ones or oatmeal."

They ate supper. The late afternoon sun flickered in through the small-paned windows. The white ruffled curtains swayed in and out. Betty pounded her mug and spoon on the shelf of her high chair and said, "Der-scher-scher," and a great many other moist, blubbery things. There was peace in the little dining room like the tranquillity of still waters, like the calm of the forest primeval, like the dulcet, melting tones of the voice that breathed o'er Eden.

Betty grew quiet, and her head rolled and jerked about from side to side. The two watched her in amused silence until she slept. Then they waited a few minutes to make sure she was all gone. It was Bob who picked her up. "Poor little tad!" he murmured in tender tones. "Papa's own little tired girl!" There is nothing so soothing to rested nerves as the implication from a paternal parent that the dear baby belongs only to its father.

Together they peeled off her clothes, stopping suddenly at the slightest show of animation on her part. By dint of much twisting and turning of plump little arms and legs they succeeded in getting her into her nightgown. Bob carried her into the bedroom and Mabel tiptoed behind him. Together they pulled the sheet over her and adjusted the shades. Together they hung over her bed and looked at each other rapturously as she gave one of those sudden fleeting smiles in her sleep that sentimental parents say are caused by the kisses of the guardian angel in its vigil, and practical physicians say are caused by kinks from a slight inflammation in the intestines.

Mabel went out to clear off the table. She had an exquisite, warm sensation that everything in the universe was right. A poet has called it "the lift of the heart."

She washed the few dishes. Never again, she thought, would she let the work get so far behind. She would, of course; but housekeepers' resolutions, like hope, spring eternal in the human heart.

When the dishes were finished, it occurred to her that Bob had not come out of the bedroom. So she went to the door and looked in. He had a yardstick in his hand with which he seemed to be measuring. Mabel watched him curiously. He cautiously moved the big bed out and then Betty's bed, measuring them both and the wall space between.

"*What* are you doing?" she whispered.

Bob wrote something down, then stuck his pencil behind his ear and said, "By George! I'm going to make the new little bed myself. I've been examining Betty's — twenty dollars for it is a frost. I'll bet I can make one and enamel it, and you can't tell the two apart."

A glow like sunshine on opals came into Mabel's face. There is a look like it on the face of Maillart's "Madonna of the Waves."

Earnest, businesslike, Bob went on. "He'll have to have one, you know. He'll have to have a bed of his own."

The madonna glow gave place to a roguishly mischievous expression: "That's so. She can't sleep with Betty, can she?"

Bob caught the inference immediately and sent back, "I should say he won't want to sleep with his sister."

Being a woman, Mabel had the last of the dialogue, "Well, she'll like her new bed, anyway, Daddy."

Bob tossed the yardstick on the bed, came up to Mabel and put his arm around her. "Gee, Mabel! It's nice to be home again alone — just you and I and Betty." He cupped his hand under the girl's chin and turned her sweet face up to him. His own dark head bent to her. "I kind of enjoyed being at the folks' again for a day or two — but after that I sure wanted to come back home. They're the *noisiest bunch!*" Bob was saying this, Bob who was "all Mason." "Marcia clatters like the bell at a railroad crossing, and Eleanor — did you ever see much a whirling dervish in your life? I like my sisters all right, but, for everyday living, I'd rather have you . . . and this cozy home . . and Betty . . . and —" he grinned boyishly down at her, he was only a grown-up boy after all — "and Betty's little *brother*." It ended in a kiss, a kiss straight from the heart of a man who loved.

The tide had come in, the magie tide that made of the little home an enchanted castle with towers and turrets of arabesque. Ah, well! Because of dreary winter, the robin's song seems more blithe and gay and lilting. And it is worth years of exile just to have the blissful rapture of coming home again.

Two blocks away, a plump lady with graying hair was saying to a tall man, apropos of nothing, "Henry, to be real honest with ourselves, don't you think, in these twenty-seven years, you and I have managed to get along remarkably well?"

Henry, who was used to being disturbed when he was reading, did not even look up.

He only said, "Well, I *have* got an unusually good disposition."

At which the plump lady made a face and said, *"Oh, you get out!"*

CHAPTER IX

JUNIOR EMULATES SIR GALAHAD

It was during the middle of this summer that Junior's natural dislike for Isabelle Thompson developed, possibly because of the extreme hot weather like any other epidemic among carnivora, into a sort of boyish hydrophobia.

The Thompsons were the Masons' nearest neighbors, the two yards being separated by a low hedge. The family consisted of Mr. and Mrs. Tobias Thompson, and two daughters: Blanche, who was a little older than Eleanor Mason, and Isabella, aged eleven.

Mrs. Thompson was a little thin woman who reveled in the reputation of being the neatest housekeeper in Springtown. Why do those characteristics so often go together? Does the thin, wiry condition of a woman's body beget neatness! Or does she keep herself worn thin by her energetic scrubbing? Is it a physiological or a psychological problem?

However that may be, Mrs. Thompson continued to lay strips of rag carpet over her best rugs to keep them clean, and then a layer of newspapers over the rag carpet to save that, too. Andy Christensen declared that she came clear out to the gate to meet him whenever he brought up the groceries on a muddy day.

Her neatness extended to the other members of her household. Tobias was proprietor of a combined grocery and meat market; and no pig, dizzily hanging head downward from its peg in the back room, looked more pink or slick or skinned than he.

"It is certainly nice to think our meat comes from such a clean place," Mother often said.

"Yes," the frank Marcia agreed, "if you don't mind a little thing like underweight."

"Believe me!" Eleanor added. "Tobias would pinch a wienie in two if he dared."

Mrs. Thompson's mind was as neat as the rest of her. It, too, was a prim, tidy place with symmetrical shelves on which were stored a few meager but immaculate items, such as cleanliness being next to godliness, dancing a device of the devil, and that the only route to heaven was via the particular church to which she belonged. Yes, everything in her mind and heart was small and neat and necessary. Those organs were not all cluttered up with a lot of unessential rubbish like Mother Mason's. There were no tag ends of emotion over the moon swinging out from behind a swirl of silver clouds, nor messy scraps of thrills because a thrush was singing in a rain-drenched lilac bush at twilight. Mother's was the soul of a poet. Mrs. Thompson's was the soul of a polyp.

She was one of the few people who riled Mother through and through. She would say, "*I* won't quarrel with any of my neighbors," as though the others ran around seeking trouble. Or, "*I've* always said honesty was the best policy." It was as though she felt she had invented honesty.

The Masons, among themselves, always spoke of the elder Thompson daughter as "Blonche," in imitation of the broad and stilted pronunciation her mother used. As for Isabelle, Junior's crowd of boys had a pet name for her also. There is a portion of the human anatomy that is never mentioned in a drawing-room. The said section is bounded on the north by the lungs, on the south by the hip-bone socket and on the east and west by the ribs. Although it is never spoken aloud in polite society, far be it from any one to accuse Junior and Runt Perkins and Shorty Marston of constituting polite society. So in the privacy of their own crowd they always spoke of the younger Thompson girl as Is-A-Belly. It was not gallant nor was it kind, but twelve-year-old boys are quite often neither gallant nor kind.

As a consequence of their mother's narrow attitude, the two Thompson girls were self-consciously engrossed in their own attainments. Their mother believed that her daughters, like the king, could do no wrong, a view that was thoroughly shared by the girls themselves. They were perfect in their manners, immaculate as to their persons, flawless in their conduct. But, lacking a sense of humor which would otherwise have been their redeeming quality, they were excellent specimens of that despicable creature — a prig.

The fun-loving Mason girls spoke always of "Blonche" as The Perfect One, and Junior continued to use that nameless, ungallant appellation for Isabelle whenever his boyish disgust of her pure, faultless record grew too deep.

Boys of this age live on the border between childhood and adolescence. It is a sort of No Man's Land in which they seem not to know just where they belong. In this they are not unlike the maiden with reluctant feet. They are such a queer mixture of youth and childhood that one hour, with developing mind, they seem to be reaching out into the future to wrestle with man-sized problems, while the next hour, with no conscious understanding of the change, they abandon that mood to drop back into the trifling plays of babyhood.

This was an hour, this particular warm summer evening, when Junior had slipped back into babyhood. With all the inanity of which he was capable, he had pried off a loose slat in the trellis-work under the back porch, and with much grunting and wiggling, had managed to crawl through. His reason for doing it? Ask the wind or the stars or the morning dew. No, the motives of a twelve-year-old boy are not always governed by a rational cause. He just did it.

Scrounging under the porch, he looked around in the semi-darkness. His eye lighted on an old battered, rusted, tin street car, a relic of younger, if not happier, days. He succeeded in pulling off one of the tin wheels. There was a hole in the center of the wheel left by the withdrawing of the hub. He held it to his mouth and blew. It gave forth a weird, plaintive sound like the mewing of a cat. Immediately, with that ability to become all things to all men, Junior felt himself taking on the characteristics of a cat. Fur seemed, in some miraculous way, to spring out on his body. With the erstwhile street car wheel between his teeth and emitting continuous purring sounds, he pad-padded out from under the porch. With that capacity for sinking himself in an imaginary character, he felt in his heart all the sly, treacherous attributes of a cat. Nay, more, he *was* a cat.

Out on the lawn he crawled through the grass of the side yard to the hedge, stopped to rub a pair of invisible whiskers against a weed, nibbled daintily at a stalk of catnip, and settling back on his haunches, laid the street car wheel aside to lap a presumably clean tongue over a slightly soiled paw. Then, with half-human, half-feline promptings, he cogitated plans for the rest of the evening.

Across the hedge at the Thompson home, some one was sitting in the hammock behind the vine-covered lattice work of the porch. Junior could hear the steady squeak-squeak of the swaying ropes. It would be Isabelly, curled and beribboned, daintily holding her big doll, likewise curled and beribboned. Just what there is in the contemplation of an immaculately clean, piously good little girl to rouse the ire of a semi-soiled, ungodly, little boy, is one with the mysteries of the Sphinx and the Mona Lisa smile. Junior, at thought of Isabelle sitting placidly in the hammock, was seized with an uncontrollable desire to startle her out of that state of calmness into one of sudden agitation.

So he crept through an opening in the hedge into the Thompson yard, pausing with an imaginary distended tail, to crouch and spring at a robin in the grass. Failing to capture his prey, he crawled noiselessly toward the porch, placed his forepaws on the lattice-work and emitting a low whining purr, peered through the vines.

It was not Isabelle. it was Blanche. In the hammock with her sat Frank Marston, his arm casually thrown across the back of the hammock, his face in close proximity to hers.

The cat did not purr again. Open-mouthed, he took in the little scene before him, which spectacle included the placing of a hasty, boyish kiss on Blanche's cheek. Then the leading man and lady both giggled rather foolishly. They were very young.

Once again in the annals of history had curiosity killed a cat, for all feline characteristics immediately left the onlooker, and he became a normal twelve-year-old masculine biped.

He slipped noiselessly away, waiting until he had turned the corner of the Thompson house before he allowed the pent-up laughter within him to trickle forth. It was too rich for words that he had witnessed it. Wouldn't every one laugh when he told them! He ran down the Thompson's side terrace, walked nonchalantly across the street and around the next block. On the way, he told the joke to three people, Runt Perkins and Hod Beeson and Lizzie Beadle. The reason that he told no one else was the very simple one that those were all the people he met.

Reaching home by this circuitous route, he burst it upon the family with the tale.

"With my own eyes I seen 'em," he finished breathlessly.

"Saw them," corrected Katherine, didactically.

"Saw 'em," Junior repeated.

If Katherine was concerned with Junior's manner of speaking, Mother was immediately concerned with the moral aspect of his spying, but Marcia and Eleanor thought only of the news.

"*What* do you know about that?" It was Marcia.

"Blonche, the fair, Blonche, the lovable,
Blonche, the lily maid of Astolot!"

"Mrs. Thompson would have a fit and fall in it." Katherine, too, was growing interested.

"I wonder if Frankie was all scrubbed and sterilized," Eleanor put in.

"Girls! Girls!" Mother remonstrated.

"Young folks are 'most all fools," was Tillie's affable contribution. At which Marcia and Eleanor wrung their hands and pretended to weep.

"Junior!" It was Mother who spoke severely. "You probably meant no harm, but let this be a lesson to you about sneaking up on any one. Promise me you'll not ever tell a soul."

"I promise," Junior said glibly. But even as he spoke he cast a guilty thought at the gossip he had left behind him like the long tail of a Chinese kite.

The next night, the Mason family had just finished supper, for in Springtown one eats dinner as the sun crosses the meridian and supper as it sinks down behind the elms that line the distant banks of old Coon Creek.

Chairs were pushed back. Tillie had begun to pick up the dishes. Father was opening the evening paper. The white ruffled curtains swayed in and out. The girls were humming in concert "Somewhere a Voice is Calling." It was as peaceful a scene as the Arcadian village of Grand Pré.

Just then the voice called, but it was neither tender nor true. It came in clicking, indignant tones from Mrs. Thompson at the dining room door. She came in like a hawk in a chicken yard. In angry tones she told them that Blonche had just heard what Junior had been telling around town about her, that there was not one word of truth in it, and that she wanted something done about it. On and on she went, delivering vindictive verbal upper-cuts to Junior, making a self-righteous speech on the excellent quality of her girls' upbringing, and finished with "Neither one of *my* girls would allow a thing like that."

For one brief, fleeting moment, Mother had an unholy desire to retort, "Oh, of course, I've *taught my* girls to spoon."

During the onslaught the members of the family had remained rooted to their respective places like the king's family during the curse on the Sleeping Beauty. When she had finished, the spell broke. Father was the first to stir. He stirred himself so thoroughly that he slipped quietly out of the dining room into the kitchen. He could have diplomatically refused a loan to the governor. He could have argued violently with the members of the state banking board. He might even have unflinchingly faced a masked bank robber. But he could not face his little angry neighbor. Mother, in exasperation, sometimes wondered how so successful a business man could be so helpless in domestic crises.

So it was Mother who took the stage. She questioned Junior. The latter, fiery red and visibly embarrassed, wanted nothing in the world so much as that the painful scene should end, even as that older masculine member of the family. So he did what almost any little boy would have done, what George Washington might have done, had there been twelve feminine eyes gazing at him in grief or anger or concern. He lied.

"I was just —" he mumbled, "just jokin'."

"You mean," Mother asked coldly, "that you made it up?"

Junior nodded his head. And his guardian angel, in sorrow, probably made a long black mark in The Book.

"Then," said Mother calmly, "you will go to every person you told and try to make right your *very poor* joke." She assured Mrs. Thompson that they would do all in their power to rectify matters, and that Junior would apologize to Blanche. Mrs. Thompson was mollified. She simpered a little. "You know *me*, Mrs. Mason. *I* don't like neighborhood quarrels."

"Neither do I," said Mother dryly.

Mrs. Thompson, in a state of mental satisfaction, wrapped her mantle of self-complacency about her and left.

"The old polecat!" Tillie remarked sweetly when the door closed. Although Tillie found plenty of fault with the Mason children, herself, let some outsider do it and she was immediately on the warpath.

Every one was perturbed. "Who did you tell?" Katherine demanded, and the fact that she did not say "whom" was proof positive that she was upset.

"I happened to tell Lizzie Beadle," Junior whimpered.

"Good *night!*" Eleanor threw up her hands. "You might just as well have put it on the front page of the Springtown *Headlight.*"

They all talked to him at once. Katherine gave a hurried résumé of the poem that concerns shooting arrows and words into the air. It was all very hard on his nerves. So he got his cap and started to the door. Action, even if it were attempting to pick up spent and scattered arrows, seemed highly preferable to the society of the super-critical women of his household.

Strangely enough it was Marcia who followed him out onto the porch. There were tears in her eyes. Careless, tender-hearted Marcia had impulsively erred so often herself that she felt more sympathy for her little brother than any one else did.

"Junie!" She threw an arm around his shoulder. "You're like a knight of old — why, Junie, you're Sir Galahad. You're going on your white horse in search of the Holy Grail, only this time the Grail is Truth."

It pleased Junior's fancy. His drooping head lifted a little. He ran down the steps and by the time he had unhitched an invisible white charger with gold trappings, mounted him and started down the street, he was quite impressed with the nobility of his journey.

Sustained by the thought of the character he was impersonating, he stopped at Thompson's and mumbled a hasty apology to the red-eyed Blanche. It was noticeable that neither the maker of the apology nor the recipient looked directly at the other.

He went next to Hod Beeson's. It was rather trying to explain his errand to him, Hod not knowing what Junior was talking about as he had let the scandal go in one coal-grimed ear and out the other. Eventually, Hod closed the rambling confession with "All right, sonny. That's all right."

So Junior rode next to the Beadles' little weather-beaten house and told fat, untidy Lizzie his message. Lizzie looked disappointed over the news. Perhaps she was thinking of a few arrows about it she, herself, had shot into the air. But she said, "You're some kid, Junie, to take all that trouble for a smartie like Blanche Thompson. Have a cookie."

Junior, further impressed with his praiseworthy conduct, rode on to the Perkins' where he made known his errand to Runt and his mother.

"Now, look at that," Mrs. Perkins turned to her own offspring. "What a gentlemanly thing for Junior to do!"

After this Junior hated to give up his holy mission. It seemed uninteresting to turn around and go home after so few visits. So he began telling other people what he was doing. He told several of the boys of his crowd and Mrs. Hayes and the Winters' hired girl. He stopped Grandpa McCabe on the street and explained his self-abasement to that deaf old man. Grandpa couldn't sense it, but gathering that something was wrong at the Thompsons', he stopped in front of their home and leaned a long time on his cane, looking anxiously toward the house.

After that, with sudden inspiration, it struck Junior that no one had mentioned his apologizing to Frank. Surely that was an oversight on his mother's part. Did not one owe an apology to the kisser just as much as to the kissee?

So he rode up to the Marstons' colonial home, dismounted and went in. The Marstons were eating dinner as Springtown people do when they have company from the city. There was a rich uncle there and his pretty daughter, to say nothing of a charming friend she had brought with her. Nicky and Frank and Shorty all sat at the table clothed in their best suits and manners.

Junior, standing humbly just inside the dining room door, cap in hand, felt that here before so appreciative an audience, was opportunity for the grand climax of his self-humiliation. So, in the polite tones of a well-bred boy, he respectfully apologized to Frank. It could not have been done with more deference or Chesterfieldian grace. Junior had a swift desire that his parents and sisters might have witnessed it.

A dull, brick red color surged over Frank's long, lean face. "What you talkin' about, kid?"

Junior dropped the rather formal, stilted tones of his former speech and dropped into his own familiar boyish ones. He seemed deadly in earnest. Any one hearing him could not help but be impressed with his sincerity. "You know, Frank, last night when you kissed Blanche Thompson — didn't you hear a cat mew? Why, Frank, it wasn't a cat. It was me. I'm going around to all the neighbors apologizin' for sayin' I seen you."

Amid smiles from the guests, an embarrassed laugh from his mother, and unrestrained shouts from his dearly loved brothers, Frank got up. Junior sensed the fact that he was to pass out with Frank, also. Not every one is gifted with as delicate and acute sensibilities.

Out in the hall Frank grabbed his caller's shoulders in a crab-like pinch. Words hissed through his clenched teeth. These were the words: "I'd like to make *you* into *mincemeat.* You hike out of here and keep your mouth shut. Ja understand? Now, *scoot!*"

It was trying to Sir Galahad to have his high mission so misunderstood. He started home a little wearily, trying to forget Frank's baneful attitude and remember only those who had praised him. Of such is the kingdom of optimists.

The entire Mason family was ensconced on the front porch. They greeted him rather effusively. Every one seemed in a softened mood toward him. The truth was, the brave way in which he had faced the results of his ill-advised joke appealed to them all.

He sat down in the hammock by Katherine, who put her arm around him. It made him hot and uncomfortable but he stood it. Marcia threw him a smile and Eleanor gave him a stick of gum. He preferred the latter. Smiles are fleeting, but gum, with proper hoarding, lasts a week. Mother spoke to him cheerfully. Even Tillie neglected to look for dirt on his shoes. Father, his feet on the porch railing, gave a long rambling speech about veracity, a sort of truth-crushed-to-earth-Abraham-Lincoln monologue.

The family went to bed with that light-hearted feeling which comes after a painful domestic crisis has been passed. It was apparent to all, that Junior, in spite of the poor taste of his joke, had vindicated himself.

And the evening and the morning were the third day.

The members of the family straggled into breakfast one by one. Mother sighed as she saw them. She knew that the ideal way was for all the chairs to be pushed back from the table simultaneously. But she could remember just once when it had happened: the Sunday morning the bishop had been there.

Junior was the last to arrive. Several drops of water, creeping lingeringly down the side of his face, proclaimed to all who were inclined to be pessimistic that he had washed. He sat down with great gusto.

"Well, I hope old lady Thompson feels better now. Ya, I sure hope she does." He chuckled, spreading eleven cents' worth of butter on a griddle cake. "The old lady was purty excited, she was. 'N so was Blonchie, 'til I fixed it all up fine about her'n Frankie. Ya, I fixed 'em. But don't you fergit it, no matter what I said last night, just the same, I *seen* 'em."

There was silence in the Mason dining room. Every one looked at Mother. Mother looked across at Father, sitting there in all his financial capableness and his domestic inability. Father looked helplessly back. Mother knew that she was expected, as usual, to take the steering wheel, but she felt like a skipper on an uncharted sea.

A son of hers had spied upon his neighbors, gossiped, and then lied about the truth. Was the falsehood of last evening a double-dyed sin? Or was it the spirit of knighthood — that gallant thing that has been handed down through the ages — the traditional honor with which a gentleman protects a lady's name? Mother gave it up. For the life of her, she did not know.

Junior, conscious of the impressive silence, decided that he was making a hit. And as it was not often given to him to create that kind of stir in this particular circle, he waxed visibly in pleased importance and genially reiterated: "Ya, no matter what I said, you can put this in your pipe — I seen 'em."

"Saw them," corrected Katherine mechanically, from pure force of habit.

"Saw'm," repeated Junior, also from force of habit, and again a pregnant silence descended upon the breakfast table.

It was broken by Father. The assembled Masons looked at him expectantly as he cleared his throat, preliminary to speech. It was a desperate situation that could rouse Father to grip the domestic steering wheel. In

Mother's expression, relief struggled with anxiety as to just what he was going to do. If he was going to thrash Junior — She half opened her lips, as Father gave another preliminary cough. Then he spoke.

"Looks a little like rain," he said. "Hope we don't have a wetting before the haying's over."

CHAPTER X

Once more summer dropped subtle hints to the Mid-West that she was about to slip away, insinuated it with cooler nights, a day or two of flurrying leaves and gay little taunts of wild asters thrown along the banks of old Coon Creek.

This meant bringing down the trunks again from the storage room that Katherine might go back to her second year of conscientious teaching in Miles City, and Marcia might try her wings in Capitol City. Keith Baldridge was anxious to be married, but Katherine wanted one more year of teaching. This love of hers was so wonderful that she wanted to hold it close a little longer as one gloats over a rare jewel before wearing it. Hesitatingly she tried to explain this to Marcia.

"Silly!" was Marcia's frank comment. "If I loved a man like that, believe me, I can see myself continuing to eat chalk and perspire over the causes of the Civil War." Yes, Marcia was different from Katherine. Never would she be afraid to face life.

And she could not quite forget that day in the spring. It had stood out cameolike, would always stand out, unbelievably lovely to her. It was the first time in her life she had ever kept anything from Mother. But she, who was usually so voluble, could not bring herself to discuss the fragile thing which had scarcely lived before it died. When she said good-by to the family, if she clung a little longer to Mother than usual, it was because she felt that Mother, with no definite information, still understood.

Arrived at Capitol City, Marcia went immediately to the room she had engaged at the Preston boarding house where several of her old sorority friends lived. There, too, lived Miss Hill, an old teacher in the Springtown schools who was now the principal of the Lafayette School in which Marcia was to teach. None of these knew that she had even met the new superintendent.

She found the girls had gone to a general teachers' meeting at the high school auditorium and so in her eleventh-hour way of doing things, she managed to breeze into the assembly room just as the final electric bell sounded. She had only time to wave her hand across the room to her old friends and to give

Miss Hill an impetuous hug.

"Hilly, I'm gladder'n anything to see you. Sit in front of me and let some of your intellectual rays shine on me, and the new supe will think I'm a handy volume of the encyclopedia."

As the electric bell ceased jangling, the new superintendent opened the door of his office suite and came briskly onto the platform. To Marcia's mortification she could feel the color drop away from her face and then return with interest on the principal.

He was speaking. "We want the keynote of the year's work to be coöperation. Coöperation among pupils, teachers, parents and superintendent."

Marcia only half heard. She was thinking about a river and a bank of moss, a few early May-blossoms and a lavender-and-gold sunset. Stray phrases occasionally penetrated her dreaming: "developing the child's initiative" or "mental, moral, and physical growth." They were as the tinkling of far-off raindrops. It was only at the close of his professional talk when announcements were made, that she roused herself.

"There are three late changes," his familiar voice was saying: "Miss Short of the third grade, Lowell, is transferred to the third grade, Whittier. Miss Miner of third grade,

Whittier, is transferred to fourth at Lowell. Miss Mason of first grade, Lafayette, is transferred to first grade, Longfellow."

All other things were suddenly forgotten in the fact that she was to go to the Longfellow School, to leave Miss Hill. Why, he had *promised* her the Lafayette grade. She had counted on Miss Hill's guiding hand.

"Oh, Hilly," she moaned, "why has he done that?"

"I don't know, dear. Go up and talk to him. Perhaps he would arrange it some other way."

Marcia's eyes snapped. "Not in four hundred years!"

"Then I'll go." And Miss Hill shouldered her portly self through the maze of chattering teachers.

Marcia looked about wildly for a chance to escape without passing that tall figure ensconced by the door. But after all she might as well walk up and face the music. It was impossible to keep out of his way for any length of time. "He will probably say 'I've met Miss Mason' and some of the girls will hear him, so I'll have to make some sort of an explanation," she thought.

Several of her friends stopped her for greetings. They were still with her when she went on to speak to the superintendent. As she came up to him he was holding out his hand as he

191

had held it out to dozens of other teachers before her.

"*This* is Miss Mason," said dear Miss Hill in her kind, cordial way.

Marcia raised eyes that were meant to be indifferently pleasant but which only succeeded in being carefully miserable. There was an awful moment — it seemed fully a quarter of an hour long.

And then — "Miss Mason?" he repeated interestedly. "Then you are one of those transferred, are you not?"

"I believe so," she said stiffly — and it was over!

She slipped away to her boarding house as quickly as she could and threw herself in a crumpled heap on the bed. "How *could* he?" she moaned. "How could he act that way after last spring?" It was horrible that she was here. If she could only get a job a thousand miles away! But school positions do not hand on gooseberry bushes as late as September.

Suddenly she thought of something. It brought her bolt upright, clutching the spread. Of course — the *girl* — the girl he had been fond of as a friend! He had decided to marry her — was engaged to her now. But even so, why couldn't he have referred to their short acquaintance like a human being? She wouldn't have mooned around and talked to him about it, just a casual reference to it and they could have dropped it. She hoped she knew her place.

The door opened below and she heard the gay voice of Inez Walker, the sorority sister who was to be her roommate. She was busily unpacking when Inez breezed in.

"Oh, Marcia, you dear thing! If you knew how like Connie Talmadge you look in that suit! Isn't he the *gorgeous* man? I'm simply overcome. Did you ever see a grander profile and *what* do you know about his not being married?"

Marcia slammed a dresser drawer. "Inez, I might as well tell you on the start — I hate him."

"Oh, Marcia, just because he transferred you? But that's nothing against *him*. What are you to *him*? Just a cog in the machinery — just a checker on his checkerboard. Now, *me* — I'd do anything he asked. If he smiled at me in that wonderful way and said: 'Miss Walker, I'm asking you to be janitor of Whittier,' I'd say: 'I'd love it! I'd rather sweep for you than teach any day!' "

And so on through the dinner time it went, the praises of the new superintendent. "He has splendid executive ability," said Miss Hill.

"He has the best looking clothes," was Rose

193

Raymond's verdict.

"*Absolutely* the most heavenly smile and *also* a magnificent jaw," contributed Inez Walker.

"Slush and *also* piffle!" said Miss Marcia Mason dryly.

Miss Hill's interview with the head of the school had availed naught. Miss Mason was to be transferred, he had told her, with his "heavenly smile." So Monday morning saw the very unusual sight of a semi-sulky Marcia, trudging with her schoolroom gods, over to the Longfellow. She had said good-by to Miss Hill, whose tears had run down her plump cheeks, and she was being met at the Longfellow by Miss Neiderhauser with the grim statement — "I hope you understand that I require my teachers to keep their plan books strictly up to date." There are principals and principals.

In the hall she saw the new superintendent. She tossed him an airy little nod to which he responded pleasantly: "Getting settled, Miss Mason?"

"Yes, thank you," said Miss Mason coolly.

So, the moving finger having writ the seasons of the year, moved on. The year was not unpleasant, for Marcia was the kind that would dig happiness out of the ruins of any catastrophe, but for some reason, life seemed to have lost its exquisite flavor. Nicky Marston dropped in occasionally on Sunday, coming over from Miles City where he was working, and was welcomed like a message from home. On the professional side Marcia nursed her pupils through Columbus chills, Thanksgiving and Christmas fevers, and a siege of Eskimo life. She brought them safely out of the valentineitis into a convalescent period of robin redbreasts and bursting lilac buds. Her relations with the superintendent remained very businesslike, very courteous, and very cool.

"I wish I could get a position next year in Honolulu or Honduras or Hongkong," she said one evening to the other girls in the boarding house.

"You'll have to decide right away tomorrow whether you'll stay or not," Rose Raymond informed her. "For the cat was on the mat to-day with the paper for next year's signatures."

It is well to insert here for the uninitiated that in all well managed schools there is some statement by which it becomes known to the teachers that the superintendent has arrived in the building. The teacher who first sees him descending like a wolf on the fold, passes the delicate and somewhat upsetting information on to the others. So, if you are a superintendent and chance to meet a small boy tiptoeing about from room to room, carrying a scrap of paper on which is scrawled "Scotland's burning," the chances are that there is no conflagration whatever, but that the expression has reference to your untimely arrival in the building. The particular sentence by which the Capitol City, Nebraska, teachers knew that the superintendent had hung his hat in the principal's office, was the time-honored and concise statement "The cat is on the mat." So when Rose Raymond said the cat was on the mat that day with the paper for next year's signatures, Marcia knew that the time had come for her to pass in her resignation.

"All right, let the cat come," she said tartly to the others. "I'm ready for him, and when I tell him I'm not signing, I shall proceed to relieve my mind of a few other things too."

"Still peeved over your transfer, aren't you, Marcia?" Inez Walker asked sympathetically. "Now, *me* — I'd wash the Whittier windows for Mr. Wheeler if he asked me to."

"Oh, *you*," said Marcia acridly, "*you'd* eat oats out of his hand."

Spring arrived, bag and baggage, the next day. She opened the schoolroom windows and blew warm breaths of mellow earth and opening buds into the room. Marcia wore immaculate white in honor of the arrival.

The kindergartners had just started home, each carrying the smudgy portrait of a distraught blue jay, when one little girl returned to knock on Marcia's door and say: "Mith Thmith thent me back to thay the cat ith on the mat." She shrilled it out just as Mr. John Wheeler, close behind her, came briskly up to the door.

"What is it?" he asked.

"Oh, nothing — they've found Mamie Jones's kitty," Marcia fibbed hastily and had the grace to blush.

"I'll be back to see you a little later, Miss Mason," "the cat" said in his businesslike way as he started upstairs.

Marcia's pupils had gone when he returned. Marcia, herself, was at the blackboard in the far corner of the room coloring a mass of lavender and green lilac sprays. Although he stepped firmly down the length of the room she seemed not to hear him until he came quite close.

"Well, Miss Mason," he was tapping the folded paper for signatures against his hand, "are you signing with us for another year?"

Marcia filled in a green leaf carefully. "No," she said coolly, "I'm not."

John Wheeler stood a moment looking down at her. Then "Why are you resigning?" he asked pointedly.

She looked up at him for a fleeting, miserable glance. "If you *must* know," she said, half frightened, "and want me to tell you truthfully, it's because the year hasn't been any too pleasant. You've not —" she was attempting to speak indifferently and was not succeeding very well, "You've been — you've picked on me," she finished lamely in a little tragic voice for the tears were very near the surface.

" 'Picked on you'? I? 'Picked on you'?" He repeated the childish phrase in supreme astonishment.

"Yes," she affirmed stoutly. "You seem to have found it necessary to transfer me against my wishes . . . and to haunt this building to criticize me . . . and to require me to hand in lesson plans when no one else did . . . and . . ." Her voice trailed off to nothing.

"So, I've haunted this building, have I? I transferred you, did I? I've criticized you, have I? I've asked you an unnecessary number of times for plans, have I?"

"What *is* this?" Marcia asked with the first trace of her old mischievousness. "That psychology exam you were going to give us?"

"No," he said hotly, "it isn't. But I'll take pains to make it clear to you what it is. Good heavens! I've haunted this building because you were in it. I transferred you so I could see you every day. Every morning this year at eight-fifteen I've locked my office door and tiptoed to the window like a High School boy and watched you go by. If I've criticized you, it was to keep the others from seeing what I supposed was written all over me. I've asked you to hand in lesson plans just to see your handwriting. I've been loony enough to think you might write something in them or on the margin to me. I've walked past your boarding house evenings. . . ." He gave a short, dry laugh. "When that first teachers' meeting was over last fall I couldn't think of anything but that you were there in the crowd. Then you came up like a small iceberg, and not only wouldn't mention ever having known me, but made it so apparent that I was not to mention it either — and all year —" He walked over to the window and stood looking out.

Marcia stole a surreptitious glance at his back but hastily resumed her task when he turned.

He came back to her. "I suppose there's only one thing it means. You're going to marry that Marston chap, are you?"

Marcia raised big, astonished eyes. "*Nicky?*" she asked incredulously. One corner of her mouth dimpled in as she bent to fill in another green leaf. "Oh, no," she said quite casually. "I'd no more think of marrying

Nicky than I would think of marrying Santa Claus."

"But Junior told me you were going to!"

"Junior said *that?*" There were only three words in the short sentence, but there was compressed into it all the big-sister exasperation that had accumulated in twelve years. Wide-eyed, unspeaking, she stood looking up at John Wheeler. Then abruptly she turned to color another leaf.

"*Don't* do another one of those things," said John Wheeler irritably. He took the green chalk from her hand and fired it into the chalk-tray.

"It develops the child's aesthetic nature," Marcia informed him cheerfully, reaching for the color. But the man caught her hand. "Marcia, didn't that day — that wonderful, unforgettable day by the river — mean anything to you?"

"Did it?" she repeated. "Well, at least enough so that when *you* didn't mention it, made it so very apparent that *I* was not to, and acted like a — a cold-storage plant all winter — I was quite wretched."

"You care!" he challenged her, tilting her face upward. but she would not look at him.

"I — don't think so."

"You do care, Marcia. You care — like I care."

For a fleeting moment she lifted mischievous eyes. "Well — of course, if it's coöperation — you want —"

He drew her to him for three wild sweet seconds.

"Oh, goodness!" she whispered, pulling herself away. "I forgot — Herbie Folsom — watering the plants."

In truth, Herbie was at that moment standing quite near, a look of deep and intense curiosity on his large fat face, the watering pot tipping perilously and spilling a steady stream down his trousers' leg.

"Herbie, you go out in the yard, and water something," Herbie's superintendent suggested.

When they were alone he took her hands again.

"Marcia . . ."

The door opened and the janitor deposited a pail, two brooms and a mop.

"Jim," said his superior officer, "I'll be busy in here for a half-hour or so. Suppose you do all the other rooms first."

"Yes, sir." Jim withdrew.

"You dear . . ."

The door was opened, and Herbie, having hastily dashed a gallon of water against the nearest tree trunk, was back ready for further exciting events.

"Herbie," said the head of the school system, "you take that watering pot, and *go home.* Water your yard until bedtime, if you want to, but *don't come back here.*"

It was nearly time for dinner to be served at Mrs. Preston's boarding house. Inez Walker, lounging in the window seat announced: "Here comes Marcia, and . . . oh, my stars and stripes forever, girls . . . *he's* walking up this way with her!"

They were all at the top of the stairs to meet her, crowding about to ask questions.

"Did you sign, Marcia?"

"No."

"Does he know why?"

"Yes."

"What did he say? Was he peeved? Does he know what you're going to do next year?"

"Oh yes, he knows." Marcia bent to her slipper to get herself in hand.

"What did he walk up this way for?"

"Oh, I don't know. I guess he was trying to find out who started that cat-on-the-mat idea."

"Does he know about *that?*" came in a chorus.

"Yes . . . I told him."

"Marcia, you *never!*"

"I did, and how Hilly worships the ground he trods, and how Rose adores his chin, and how Inez keeps a newspaper picture of him pinned on her mirror."

"Marcia!" It was Miss Hill with her most principal-y air. "Stop making up things and tell us just *what* he said to you."

Marcia faced her tormentors. "Well, if you insist upon knowing — he thinks I'm a *punk* teacher. He's advised me to get clear out of the profession, and try something else next year."

Then she went into her room, banged the door and locked it.

CHAPTER XI

FATHER RETIRES

Events moved rapidly in the Mason household, as they always do when the children reach womanhood and manhood. It is the young themselves who welcome the changes. Only the parents reach out impotent hands that would fain hold the little ones back from their journeying. One day all seems shouting and confusion and hurrying of little feet to and fro. Almost the next there is silence and peace — a silence that is stifling, a peace that is painful. It is an age-old tragedy — the Passing of the Children.

There was a double wedding of the sisters, Katherine to Keith Baldridge, Marcia to John Wheeler. "Mother," Marcia said on the wedding day, "it took Kathie over a year to know for sure she cared for Keith; but — don't you be shocked and don't you *dare* tell a soul — I could have married John *eleven* minutes after I met him."

Mother looked up, laughing. "Kathie's conservative, like Father; and you're impulsive, like me." Then she flushed to the roots of her graying hair and added, "Don't *you* be shocked, and don't *you* dare tell a soul: I knew I wanted Father long before he knew he liked me." But this is Father's chapter, neither Marcia's nor Mother's.

The wedding of the two girls was a particularly distressing event to Father. He could not think of the girls as anything but little tots. "Seems like they ought to be wearing pinafores yet," he said to Mother. He wandered aimlessly, lonesomely, around the big house on the eventful day. Only his position of host made him attempt any cheerfulness. He had nothing to do, was in the road, in fact. "Isn't there something I can help with?" he asked. "I'll do anything but wear a dress suit." There was nothing; but he stayed on doggedly, as one clings to a sinking ship.

Mother was all smiles and bustling energy. Father watched her in amazement. Was it possible she didn't care as deeply as he? Ah, Father, little you knew!

There were palms and flowers and a caterer from Capitol City. To be sure, Mother and Tillie could have baked things that tasted better; but every woman wants a caterer once in her life. The time for the ceremony came. Katherine, sweet, womanly, Madonnalike —

Marcia, flushed, starry-eyed, lovely — both visions in their white gowns and flowing veils. But something was the matter with Father's vision. He couldn't seem to see them as they appeared to the rest of the company. Katherine persisted in skipping along down the street to meet him, her smooth braids bobbing out behind her. Marcia kept pelting him with twigs and leaves, peering down roguishly from the old apple tree through a tangle of curls. There was a lump in Father's throat all evening as big as a china egg. King and banker, and ancient arrow maker, all utter the same thing: "Thus it is our daughters leave us!"

But after the girls were gone Father slipped comfortably back into the old routine, and Mother was the one who seemed to grow restless. She was tired, she said: she wished they could go away somewhere.

"Why don't you let up a little, Father?" she would ask. "You've been tied to that bank all these years, and how many vacations have you ever taken?"

"The few times I did take them," Father returned, "I was like a fish out of water."

"But it's different now," Mother protested. "You're getting old, and if any one is entitled to take things easy, you surely are."

Mother kept at him so persistently that it gradually began to seem an alluring picture to Father: not to be tied down, not to have to work any more. When Satan took the Man of Galilee up into a high mountain and showed him all the kingdoms of the world it is not recorded that he held out the delightful promise that no work would ever have to be done, but it is quite possible that this was part of the temptation.

So Father commenced to think about getting out of his harness. He was where he could take things easy if he chose. Surreptitiously he began filling the backs of old envelopes with figures, estimating what he could get from his bank stock if he sold. Other scraps of paper bore the figures of investments he would make, what his income would be. Yes, he could retire and live quite comfortably. He wouldn't sell the hundred and sixty. Like a great many men in whose veins runs the blood of pioneers, he felt more secure with a little farm land he could always fall back on.

Evenings when the two were alone he began to speak quite casually to Mother about what they could do *if* they sold. He was very conservative, was Father. It had never been his way to go off half-cocked. Mother, who was by nature an enthusiast, less level headed than Father, fairly bubbled with plans. Would they be fixed so they could afford a year of travel? It would be better for Eleanor than college, a great experience for Junior. they could close the house. Tillie could work for Bob and Mabel. And Father, figuring and figuring, said he guessed they could manage it all right. By common consent they said nothing before Eleanor and Junior. The children couldn't quite be trusted with such astounding plans until they were perfected.

So Mother got out books of travel and maps. She sent for information on personally conducted tours and found herself promptly deluged with literature. She spoke magic names glibly, names that hitherto had seemed as far removed from their lives as scenes from Arabian Nights — the Mediterranean, Venice, the Alps.

"I've dreamed of it all my life! Think of it, Father, to set out to sea — with the coast lights growing fainter — and the spray — and the sky meeting the water!"

"Yes, I'd like it too," said Father.

So Father listed the Springtown First National Bank at a topnotch price with the Van Orden Company at Miles City. And in a short time one of the Van Ordens swung around the bank corner in a big touring car with two men, a short, red-faced man and a younger one, whom he introduced as the Coles. They talked long and seriously in the little back office. Father had Bob bring in files from the various cases. Together they went over bunches of notes and mortgages. Father, in reserved, dignified pride, showed them everything. There was nothing to conceal, for there was not a five-dollar loan that was poor paper. Father's house was in order.

"It's a h— of a price," said Cole, Senior.

"It's a good bank," said Father simply.

And thereafter at any threat on Cole's part not to consider the big price, Father would reiterate: "That's the price. Take it or leave it." Father was nobody's fool.

But the whole thing began to get on his nerves. Partly from the dislike of the ranting, stamping Cole, and partly from a natural indignation at seeing a stranger assume an air of ownership in his old office, he grew tired of the deal. It irritated him whenever that big touring car swung around the corner and the men came bustling in. For they came many times. It takes longer to buy even a country bank than it does a kitchen range.

After one long session of discussion, suddenly, like a violin string snaps, Cole said he would take it. After which he swaggered about Father's office, swore a little, and spoke of changes he would make in the working policy, changes in the force, changes in the fixtures. Then, with the agreement that Father was to come to Miles City on the following Wednesday to sign the contracts, he left.

In the intervening days the transaction began to prey upon Father's mind. It was as though there yawned at his feet a deep and wide fissure in the good old earth. He did not sleep well. He minced his food — Father, who had partaken of three hearty meals a day for years. The memory of Old Man Hanson persistently haunted him — the old man in Cedar County who had sold his home farm and then committed suicide.

Mother tried several times to arouse his enthusiasm over their coming year, but, sensing his preoccupied mind, she, too, grew reserved.

He began to brood over the thing, to think of it as a colossal mistake. What would he do, he asked himself, when he returned from that year's trip? He looked across the street to where a dozen men were sitting on boxes and kegs in front of Sol Simon's store, talking, chewing, whittling. There were farmers among them who were retired and town men who were merely tired. Some were real old men. Some were — fifty-nine. Father shuddered.

Wednesday loomed before him, big and black and fiendish like the end of everything. The gates that he had persuaded himself were to swing open to Freedom seemed now to his obsessed mind to clang in upon him, prison-like. The only way that he could get out of the deal was to pay the big commission. Also, he had given his word, and the occasion had yet to occur when a man could say Henry Y. Mason had broken his word.

Tuesday afternoon, as he waited upon a few old-time patrons, he felt like a traitor to be turning these good old men over to that hot-headed, tempery Cole. The deal no longer seemed even legitimate. Benedict Arnold and Judas Iscariot had made like transactions.

When they closed up, Father lingered in his office. He felt dazed, a little sick. He couldn't just place his illness. It might be his stomach, he wasn't sure.

Bob was outside waiting for him.

"Better have a good lawyer with you, Dad," he suggested. "Judge Gumming or J. T. Neftt."

"No," said Father shortly; "I can hold my own."

Most of the night he lay awake, turning and turning. To Mother's solicitous inquiry he said irritably, "It's my corn. The one on my left foot," he added specifically.

They were both up by daylight. Mother got breakfast — buckwheat cakes and country sausage and coffee. Father was none of your grapefruit, French toast people. But he did not eat much.

"You'll come home to-night without any ball and chain," Mother said. "You'll be a free man."

"Yes," he agreed in a thin voice, and then added cheerfully for Mother's sake, "Yes, sure!"

On the way to the early morning train he stopped at the bank. As he unlocked and went in to get his little black grip with its important papers, he looked neither to the right nor the left, getting out hurriedly as one steps out from the room where the dead lie sleeping. He had an uncanny feeling that the old brick building was staring reproachfully after him. A block away he yielded to a childish desire and looked behind him. It was true. He had never noticed before how much the two big plate-glass windows looked like eyes.

On the train he dropped into a seat and stared mechanically out at the familiar water tank and lumber yard. Across the aisle two men were having a friendly argument over some minor point in the policies of National and State banks. One of them turned. "Here's Mason of Springtown," he said. "Ask him. He knows the subject like a kid's primer." Father made a half-hearted remark or two, excused himself and went into the smoker. He felt hurt, out of it.

"Mason isn't looking very fit," one of them volunteered.

"Probably breaking," the other returned. "It gets us all after a while."

At Miles City he went immediately to the Van Ordens'. In their private office were the two Van Ordens, the two Coles, two attorneys, and a stenographer. That made seven. And Father!

"Now, gentlemen, let's get right down to business." It was one of the Coles.

Father's hands and feet were as cold as ice, but his head felt clear and his mind singularly active.

The contract was being written. "We want," said Cole, "a clause whereby Mason will be required to take over any paper that we decide we want to throw out in the first six months."

"No," said Father firmly. "I won't agree to that."

"It's a legitimate proposition," said Cole snappishly.

"Rather customary," agreed one of the Van Ordens.

"A mighty small matter," put in the other Cole; "if the paper's all good."

"No," said Father doggedly. He was sighting a hole, a very small hole through which the sun was shining. If he could only get them

213

to drop it of their own accord.

Cole was getting mad. "I insist on the clause." He thumped the table. He was used to having his way, could not bear to be crossed.

Like a bulldog Father hung on grimly; "No," he repeated quietly.

The Van Ordens worked like Chinese go-betweens. They worked until they sweat. Finally Cole swore a long hyphenated oath. He stood up, red and hot. "The deal's off," he said loudly.

"All right," said Father quietly. "Deal's off."

The Van Ordens came to Father. They were sorry, apologetic. They did not blame him by any means, and they would be glad to make another deal.

"No," Father told them; "it isn't for sale now."

Father was down in the bustling street, his little weather-beaten grip held tightly in his hand. Street cars were clanging by. Boys were calling the noon edition. The sun was struggling to shine through the fog and the smoke. The old First National was still his. Only a few times in his life had he experienced this same sensation of relief from catastrophe: the time the panic so near caught him; the straightening out of an unfounded rumor that

Bob had been mixed up in a disgraceful college scrape; the time Eleanor passed the crisis in pneumonia. He looked up through the murky haze, past the tops of the tall office buildings. "Good Lord!" he ejaculated aloud. It was the nearest to a public prayer Father had ever come. He felt young. He was only fifty-nine, and he had thought of retiring! He, who had health and strength and energy, had been about to commit himself voluntarily to the rubbish pile! A dull red spread over his face. He was ashamed of himself. Ten, fifteen, twenty years from now he could quit.

He turned and with long steady strides walked down the street, out of the business section, through a park, past lovely homes, out where the houses were scattering. At the very edge of the last suburb he stopped and looked out across the wide stretch of fields and meadows, asleep now under a powdery quilt of snow. A verse of Coleridge's lying dormant in his mind, long forgotten, came suddenly to him.

And winter slumbering in the open air
Wears on his smiling face a dream of spring
I the while, the sole unbusy thing,
Nor honey make, nor pair, nor build, nor sing.

"Work is good," he said to himself.

"Work is healthful and right. It keeps men sane and well balanced. No one with health and strength should step out of the ranks. He should be, as Emerson says, 'Too busy with the crowded hour to fear to live or die.' "

For a few moments longer he stood wrapped in thought. Then hunger seized him, a good, healthy, ravenous hunger, the first he had felt in weeks. He walked rapidly back to the car line and rode downtown.

It was nearly midnight when Father got into Springtown on Number Nine. To city dwellers a train is a means of locomotion. To small-town people it is an individual. They call it "she," and speak pridefully of her when she is on time and vindictively when she is late. Father got off the Number Nine, which was only a few minutes late, and swung away up Main Street. He looked up at the stars keeping their unchanging vigil over the sleeping town. His heart was tender and he felt a yearning over all the dark old houses. He must do something for Springtown, something useful.

By the bank door he paused and then, at the risk of being mistaken for a burglar by old Sandy Wright, the night watchman, he unlocked and went in. Back in his private office he sat down at his desk and looked about him. Everything was his; the business, the fixtures, the furnishings, the very calendars. Nothing belonged to Cole — nothing. It was like the relief after nightmare. For some time he sat there, making new plans. The boys all ought to have their salaries raised. They were good boys. With a little figuring it could be done. His eyes fell upon a huge bill above the desk. It told of Henry Schnormeir's dispersion sale, scheduled for the next day. He'd clerk at that sale, himself, thought Father. He'd tell D. T. he wanted to do it.

It was not until he had locked the door and started toward home that he gave a definite thought to Mother's attitude. It struck him forcibly that Mother's disappointment would probably be keen. She had wanted to take a trip like that all her life. Well, she and the children should go, anyway. He could stay at Bob's.

Mother was still up. It was an old trick of Mother's. "Seems like I can't go to sleep comfortably until every one is in," she would say. She put up her book now and looked questioningly at Father. "Well?" She was placid, serene. "How did everything go? Did you have a hard day?"

"Oh, no, not very." Father put it off a moment longer. Then he plunged bravely in with "Well, Mother, the deal's off. Fallen through."

"Fallen through?" she repeated wonderingly. "I didn't know it *could* fall through now."

"Yes, we stuck on a clause in the contract. The old bank's still ours, and there'll be no long trip for me this year."

Suddenly, surprisingly, Mother burst into tears. Of all people to go off like that! Mother, who was not the crying kind! She was disappointed, then, to the very core. Father opened his mouth to tell her that she and the children should take the trip anyway, but Mother spoke first. "Oh, Henry," she wailed, "I never meant to b-bawl like this — but you don't know how *glad* I am. I've been just *sick* about it the last two weeks, but I never let on to you. I got to wondering if you'd be contented with nothing to do — and I got to thinking about going in a b-boat that might leak — and the family all being separated — and *Christmas* and *birthdays* — oh, I just couldn't *stand* it. A whole year! Why, *anything* might happen, Henry. Katherine or Marcia might even have a *b-baby* and their own *mother* far away. Home *never* looked so good to me."

Astonished, Father sat down limply in his big leather chair. "Can you *beat* it?" he asked faintly.

Father clerked at the Schnormeir sale. All

day long, in his old moth-eaten Galloway coat, dilapidated cap, and hip boots, he stood ankle-deep in soft mud and took the farmers' notes. In unoccupied moments he would lift his head and inhale long deep breaths of the wind that swept over the prairie, the wind that was laden with earth-odors, the good old smells of loam and clod and subsoil. It caressed his cheeks and nostrils, and whispered of the coming of purple-flowered alfalfa, and rustling corn and shimmering, swaying wheat heads. It is to the son of the prairie what the clear cold breeze from the snow-capped peaks is to the mountaineer, what the wet, salt-filled wind is to the sailor.

At night, tired, dirty, contented, Father rode home in a little mud-spattered rattling auto with two farmers, a stockman, and a railroad section hand. He was very democratic, was the president of the First National Bank of Springtown.

As he got out at home and passed around to the rear of the house, he saw Mother in the cob-house. Nearly every small-town home in the corn-bearing district possesses such a building. It is ostensibly for cobs, but also serves splendidly for a catch-all. At the sight of Mother in the doorway, Father tried desperately to conceal something down at his side. But the thing was too large. Mother glared coldly, inhospitably at it. It was a bird cage. The seed dishes were cracked. The perches were broken. A crow could have escaped through the rusty bent bars.

"Nobody bid on it," said Father sheepishly.

"Most *presumably* not," returned Mother with dry sarcasm. Then she threw back her head and laughed, a gay bubbling laugh, so that Father felt immensely relieved, and grinned too. "Never mind, Father," she spoke with mock sympathy, "I've got one old hen that wants to set. It'll be just the thing to put her in."

They were back in the old comfortable rut, the dear old routine of living. Let the discontented sail the salt seas looking for high adventure! Let the dissatisfied climb the highest peak searching for the nesting place of the bluebird of happiness! To Father and Mother Mason, adventure beckoned alluringly with every sun that rose over the far distant hooded hills and rolling prairie land. Contentment lay in the place they had made for each other and for the children. They were good folks, kind folks, simple-hearted folks — and God give us more! — to whom it would not have mattered greatly if, instead of the big comfortable house with its ample rooms and sunny porches, there had been but a poor wee hut tucked away somewhere out of the wind and rain, for with willing hands and loving hearts, they would have made of it — HOME.

The employees of THORNDIKE PRESS hope you have enjoyed this Large Print book. All our Large Print books are designed for easy reading — and they're made to last.

Other Thorndike Large Print books are available at your library, through selected bookstores, or directly from us. Suggestions for books you would like to see in Large Print are always welcome.

For more information about current and upcoming titles, please call or mail your name and address to:

THORNDIKE PRESS
PO Box 159
Thorndike, Maine 04986
800/223-6121
207/948-2962

P

AUTHOR	CLASS
ALDRICH, B S	F G

TITLE

Mother Mason